HIS BROTHER'S VISCOUNT

By the Author

Second Chance Series:

His Midshipman

His Second Chance

His Pirate

His Brother's Viscount

Florian's Garden

Thom's Desires

Visit us at www.boldstrokesbooks.com

HIS BROTHER'S VISCOUNT

by

Stephanie Lake

2021

ISBN 13: 978-1-63555-805-0

This Trade Paperback Original Is Published By
Bold Strokes Books, Inc.
P.O. Box 249
Valley Falls, NY 12185

First Edition: January 2021

CREDITS
EDITORS: JERRY L. WHEELER AND STACIA SEAMAN
PRODUCTION DESIGN: STACIA SEAMAN
COVER DESIGN BY TAMMY SEIDICK

Acknowledgments

Thanks to our fantastic beta readers, Jules Radcliffe and Andrea. Special thanks go to Keren Reed, and to the BSB team: Jerry, Stacia, and Tammy—it was a pleasure working with you for the first time on what hopefully will be many stories to come.

To our fans, who make writing worth the time, toil, rewrites, and more rewrites! Hugs!!!

PROLOGUE

Summer 1790, Kent

"You bloody, cowardly, worthless cur!" Baron Forsythe yelled, the slurred words so loud they spilled from the imposing Forsythe country home.

Tyler jumped. He heard the raging storm from the front door, where he waited for at least a minute before the blasted red-liveried footman opened the door a few inches. He pushed the man aside. The next outburst could be heard from the adjoining county, as he ran down the hallway.

"Get back here, you worthless Satan spawn, and drag your sniveling brother out from under that damn table!"

How fortuitous. He'd arrived in time. Apparently, the baron hadn't caught the boys, so he could not have beaten them. Yet. Tyler flung open the library door and heard eleven-year-old Will defying his drunkard of a father.

"Stay where you are, Heckie," Will yelled at his four-year-old brother, Hector, who scurried from one side of the table to another when his father stretched out a fat, beringed hand beneath in an attempt to catch him. The small, dark-haired boy darted as quick as a pony each time the tottering baron reached for him.

Will, standing on a ladder next to one of the bookshelves, looked for all the world like a black-haired pirate. His coat was missing, and his white shirt billowed loose about his hips. Tall boots and tan breeches completed the image. The only thing lacking was a parrot on one shoulder. He yelled when his father barely missed Hector's coat, and he lobbed book after book at the screaming, lard-filled gas bag.

The old man changed tactics and lumbered to the ladder. "Down from there, you scoundrel. If you think being my spare will save your skin from a thrashing, you can think again." The afternoon sun glared through the tall windows, momentarily blinding him as he moved closer to Hector.

Tyler bellowed, "Enough!" in an imitation of his grandfather's resounding authority, and the baron turned his small eyes on him.

"You're Wentworth's whelp, aren't you? Don't think because your grandfather's a viscount, I won't thrash you as well." Lord Gas Bag paused, grunted, and turned slowly toward Tyler. "Now I have a third impudent rascal to thrash." Another grunt and a snarling smile that revealed a row of yellow teeth.

Even though Tyler was not full grown, only two years older than Will, he had inherited his grandfather's daring. So he held his ground and stiffened his shoulders.

"Leave, young Wentworth," Lord Gas Bag said. "This matter is none of your concern." The man didn't approach Tyler, but he did stop his progress toward Will.

"I believe my grandfather would disagree, don't you, Lord Forsythe? After you broke William's arm, he will not overlook any more abuse. I do believe he told you so himself, did he not? My grandfather won't take it lightly if you lay a hand on one of his grandsons." Tyler drew himself up to his newly gained sixteen-year-old height, hoping to intimidate. "You're only a baron, after all," he added with a bold insolence.

Lord Gas Bag's piggy eyes glared. "I told you to leave, lordling. This matter is none of your concern. Your grandfather will not care about you. After all, you are not the heir, nor even the spare."

Lord Forsythe had broken Will's arm when he'd tried to stop him from beating Hector. He'd thrown Will, who fell and hit a marble step. Tyler, in London at the time with his family, was not here to help. He should have been here to protect them against the unpredictable baron. He'd neglected his friend, so he blamed himself that Will couldn't play outside for almost two months.

Gas Bag waved a hand. "As you can very well see, your grandfather is not here."

"Nonetheless, I will make certain to tell him."

Lord Forsythe turned, glared at all of them with his evil eyes, then stumbled to the door. He growled over a broad shoulder, "You overstepped your bounds this time, young man. See that you do not do so again."

The door slammed so hard, the windows rattled and a leather-bound book fell to the floor from the highest shelf.

Tyler's legs buckled under him as he dropped into a plush blue velvet chair. His head bounced on the stiff, straight back.

Will stayed on his perch, perhaps afraid his father would return, perhaps too shaken to move. "Blast it, Ty. I thought Father would murder you for sure this time."

Tyler shook his head. "No, he won't hurt me." Fortunately, his words sounded braver than he felt. "He is too afraid of Grandfather to do anything, but I think the two of you should stay with me at Wentworth Manor for a few days until he forgets what he is angry about."

With large brown eyes open so wide they were almost round, Hector slipped out from under the table and ran to Tyler. Then the impetuous boy jumped onto his lap, put both hands on Tyler's face, and kissed his cheek repeatedly with sticky, soft lips that smelled like baked apples.

Tyler laughed. "Hector, what…?"

"Love you, Tyler. Goin' to marry you when I grow big."

Will and Tyler giggled, their fear put behind them as simple as that. Tyler ruffled Hector's dark, curly hair. The mop puffed around his head like an unruly bird's nest. "Sprout, you are a silly, romantic child. Boys cannot marry boys. When you grow up, you will have to marry a girl."

Hector scrunched up his lips and kissed his cheek again. "Don' like girls. They bite."

Tyler hugged him, then stood and set him down. "Not all girls bite, silly. Just Mary Ann Pope. Now, let's pack a few things and go to my home in time for tea. Mildred is baking plum cake."

Will and Hector grinned from ear to ear as the three of them dashed out of the library and tore up the wide, curving staircase. Less than fifteen minutes later, they were running across green summer meadows with a bag full of toys and purloined sweetmeats from the kitchen.

A few times, Hector fell. Each time, Tyler helped him up, and the boy never cried. "You are a tough little man, Sprout. Perhaps you will be a soldier when you grow up."

Hector smiled at him and then ran down a hill.

"He's learned to be tough, Ty. Has to with all the things Father has done. And with Stephen off at school, Father has gotten worse."

Tyler looked at Will, realizing he was tough and brave, and for the very same reason. Damn their father to Hades.

"Thank you for coming to our rescue for the hundredth time."

Tyler rolled his eyes at the exaggeration.

"I shall pay you back someday."

"No need, Will. I'll always be there to help you. You know that."

Hector had reached the bottom of the hill and threw his little arms into the air. "I won. I won."

Will muttered under his breath, "Little urchin cheated. I didn't even know it was a race."

"Come on. Let's show him what big boys can do." They were off like a powder blast.

That night all three of them squeezed into Tyler's bed.

Tyler felt Hector smashed up against his back, holding tight. It was a little uncomfortable, but Will was the one who kept him awake all night. Will was on his back, and Tyler could see his perfect features from the moonlight streaming in the open windows—straight nose, sooty long lashes, wide mouth, ebony hair rumpled in sleep.

Tyler watched Will breathe and then swallow. Occasionally he would tense his lips into what almost looked like a smile.

That night, with new and very pleasant sensations tingling through his body, Tyler wondered why men couldn't marry other men. It seemed a pity.

Chapter One

Eighteen years later, late spring 1808, a few miles east of London

Today's journey was a fool's errand. Fourth Viscount Tyler Wentworth was not even certain why he was on this hill at this moment. Was he motivated by revenge or simple lust? Lust certainly played a part, but how much?

"My lord?" His footman had climbed from the back of the gleaming black carriage and proffered a spyglass.

He dismounted his warmblood mare, tossed the reins to the footman, and took the spyglass, given to him when he had gained midshipman status. The cool metal felt good in his hand, like it belonged there. But even that bit of comfort could not calm his riotous thoughts.

Why had he agreed to this trip? He had sworn never to be in the same county as any of the Somervilles until his cold body was safely stored in the family vault—because unfortunately, his family's crypt was adjacent to theirs.

Yet here he stood, and if all or part of his decision was motivated by revenge, then who was the target? William, Hector, himself?

All he knew was that he had been dead inside for two years. This journey would change that, for better or worse.

Given his history, things would likely get worse. The third son should never have inherited, but typhus cared not for rank. Now shouldering the title he never coveted, having lost most of his family seven lonely years ago and everyone else he loved five years later, he realized he possessed very bad luck. Very bad luck indeed.

He surveyed the verdant hills. A church spire stabbed the sun-bleached sky, a distant village smudged purple like a bruise against the landscape, and the dreariness of a skeletal gray manor house disturbed the countryside's beauty. Wentworth was close enough to the manor to distinguish a bustling crowd of garishly dressed partygoers on its vast lawn. They looked like multihued blemishes on the earth.

One of those in the party would leave with him today. The man's trunk, which arrived last night, now rested safely in the luggage compartment of the carriage. Early this morning, he'd patted the trunk's battered oak and leather surface, smiling in anticipation like a schoolboy on the first day of Christmas vacation. Now the sight of it made his stomach churn. Was he making a mistake?

He'd brought two of his finest horses for the holiday. He and his guest could travel with ease on horseback to his estate in one afternoon, but he'd also brought the coach in case they felt an urgent need for privacy. He forced away the stir of impatience.

Wiping perspiration from his brow, he raised the spyglass. The sun's angle sent harsh rays directly into his eye, momentarily blinding him. A novice's mistake he had not made in a decade. He shaded the lens with one hand, and the small round view came slowly into focus.

As bad luck would have it, he immediately spied the one

person in the world he wished never to set eyes on again. Dropping the spyglass, he closed his eyes, but it was too late. The lidded darkness showcased one potent mental image that would haunt his sleep once he laid his head to a pillow.

He remembered a closeness lost. His knees buckled, but he righted himself with a hand on the large wheel beside him. Hollowness sucked at his cold heart, jerking it back into the land of feelings, of pain. He swallowed the bile crawling up his throat and lashed out with a quick turn and a snapping left jab to the side of his carriage.

The punch landed true, but the wood proved faulty. His hand slid through a weak section, one jagged piece of pine veneer slicing his skin from thumb to wrist.

"Damnation!"

He extracted his bloody hand from the broken wood. It would hurt later, but it was surprisingly numb now.

Well, hell.

His coachman jumped off the driver's seat. "M'lord. Ye all right, m'lord?"

He waved the man aside while he stripped off his cravat. "Might as well tie Grey to the back with Dash. Difficult to hold the reins with a bandaged hand. Lot of bloody good it did to pick my best horses for the trip. The poor beasts will be choking on dust for hours."

His driver nodded, looking grave.

The irony of the situation being, in his current foul mood, there would be no need for privacy and no reason to show off by bringing his best horses.

Wrapping the cravat around his wound, he climbed into the conveyance, stewing over the image of a handsome couple kissing with babe in arms. "Bloody hell." He spat the curse with great force, as if the words alone could incinerate his misery.

❖

Hector raised his face to the warm spring sun. The gods had worked together to make this a perfect day. Well, he had a small part in making all the components align correctly, of course. He smiled, looking forward to what lay ahead.

Flourishing spring-green grass spread all the way to the surrounding forest, the manor house stood bright against a vibrant sky, and a light breeze cooled the air and carried the scent of woodbine.

He admired the spread of food arrayed on large linen-covered tables. One dish containing meat in a dark gravy filled the air with a savory fragrance that started his stomach to rumbling. The crystal, which sparkled in the sunshine, was filled with the best wines from France, and delicate porcelain tableware was arrayed for the guests' use.

Youngsters chased one another about. The light giggles of two young women and the hearty laughter of young men added to the festive air. Yes, it was a glorious day, brimming with joy, but the party alone could not explain the gale-force euphoria surging through his body.

In fact, he could not remember life ever being this enjoyable. Especially not in the past eighteen months. *Certainly* not in the past eighteen months.

His favorite—well, his only, but he knew she would always be his favorite—niece's christening had progressed along wonderfully. But his attention wandered to things other than the party. Even with the warm sun, he shivered thinking about the night to come. If he wasn't careful, he might even sport wood. Now wouldn't that be a shock to old Aunt Dorothea?

"Well, don't you look like the man who stole the raspberry

tart?" Will slapped him on the back with a bit too much enthusiasm.

Hector winced but would not let sibling rivalry ruin his day. He'd always been smaller than his two older brothers, and Will's mere presence reminded him of his deficiency.

"Careful, you might drop Pug in your attempt to collapse my left lung."

"I'd never drop my precious girl," Will cooed to the babe in his arms. "And stop calling her Pug."

He looked up at Will—two inches up, to be exact. Two very important inches. Two inches and a scar that changed common, everyday looks into the dangerously dashing Dr. William Somerville. It wasn't only size that distinguished the two of them. Will had his jaunty black hair, black eyes, and a swarthy complexion. Hector had washed-out mud brown, faded mud brown, and light mud brown.

But today it didn't matter that he was small and forgettable. Today, Hector felt like Apollo himself.

"'Fraid I cannot stop calling her Pug, old man, not until she grows into those ears of hers." He laughed at Will's puckered expression. "By the way, the celebration is going well. All the work your wife forced us into this morning paid off outstandingly."

The early hours they spent tacking up decorative paper in the high-ceilinged grand hall and around the stone balustrades made the inside and outside of the manor rather festive. They'd rearranged furniture and pinned up paper decorations for his brother's first child's first party. Margaret Harriet Philadelphia Somerville. What a designation. Will had taken leave of his senses when he labeled the poor girl with that name. But even with that taint, Pug was a sunny child with her mother's fawn-colored hair and her father's rambunctiousness. At just three months, she managed to grab everyone's attention, a little sun at the center of whatever room she occupied. It'd taken Hector two months to decide he really quite liked the girl even though she was an unsightly pink, wrinkly thing that smelled of curdled milk.

"My little girl's ears are in perfect proportion. She is beautiful." Will glowed, simply oozing fatherly pride. He acted like a simpleton around his squirming bundle, making funny squeaking noises and wiggling his fingers—as he did now—to make his daughter laugh. And she did laugh, with a toothless, infectious mirth.

Hector laughed with her and ruffled the baby's tuft of downy hair.

Will's attention, as usual, was divided between his daughter and his wife, Mary. She chatted with guests, lovely in a sunny yellow muslin afternoon dress. Mary was one of those natural beauties who were always attractive. In fact, she probably woke up pretty, even with rumpled hair, pillow marks on her cheek, and sleep in her eyes.

Anyone who glanced at them could tell that Will and Mary were besotted. That was what he wanted. He wanted someone to stay by his side, to wake up with every morning. Someone to grow old with. Someone he found beautiful even with rumpled hair, pillow-creased cheeks, and a sparkling drop of drool on silk sheets.

A stupid romantic, he, ever since boyhood; but on a day like today it was hard not to be. Because even if he didn't quite match up to his older brothers, it didn't matter. Somebody had noticed him again, and today that somebody would collect him for an extended stay in the country.

He had magnificent plans for this fortnight. He rubbed his hands together, the friction warming his fingers, getting them ready for anything. Everything. Yes, joy filled his body today, and nothing would ruin his optimism for the future. Not even his brother's perfection.

Even so, he stiffened when Will said, "You enjoy little Margaret so much, you should marry, have your own children."

"That won't happen, Will. You know why, so leave off."

Tight-lipped, Will looked about to say something. Fortunately, Mary joined them at that moment. "How are my three favorite Somervilles?" she said in her soft, smoky alto. She leaned over and kissed her daughter's forehead, then brushed the fuzzy locks back into place. She glowed with pride, just like her husband. "Hector, I believe you are as fond as we are of our little girl."

"Actually, I spent the day planning my revenge. I will take her on outings, spoil her rotten, and then give you back an overexcited and insufferable child."

Will groaned with an age-old weariness. "Save your strength. I will simply hand her off to Nanny Pennington if you do so. Besides, you've given me enough trouble throughout my lifetime. I don't need her following in your footsteps."

"Me? You were the one who tormented me to distraction and tears. And got me into predicaments where I required doctors to sew me up."

Will laughed. "I will not deny Stephen and I were terrors, but in my defense, he usually instigated the worst of the pranks."

Hector snorted but knew he'd been partly to blame, always following his older brothers, wanting to be as big, bold, and brave. They'd picked on him because he'd been the youngest, the weakest. It didn't matter. Hector no longer held animosity over his brothers' dealings. To be honest, they hadn't been that bad. They shared brotherly affection. They held together through their father's drunken abuse. In fact, Hector could remember times when Will took the switch meant for him.

He did appreciate his older siblings. It was just that sometimes, when the days were gloomy and he did not quite know what to do with his life, the comparisons to perfection rankled.

❖

The crunch of wheels on gravel alerted Will to a new arrival. He watched a sleek, black carriage pull into the circular drive. Two large, saddled horses tethered to the carriage shook their hides and bobbed their heads. One of them whinnied.

"Er, William." Hector's voice broke. "I must go. I have plans for a holiday. A fortnight out in the country. I've been in London too long. Time to stretch my legs, do a little hunting, that kind of thing, you know?"

"Why keep it a secret until now?" *What the hell?* Hector was rambling. He had an idea why he just now learned of the trip, and he felt his blood start to simmer.

"What, I didn't tell you? Been planning this for a while but didn't know if I would have time to go. Must have slipped my mind. Telling you, I mean." Hector stared at his feet.

A lie. "Where are you going? Who are you going with?"

Hector fiddled with his cravat.

"Now, Will, you are not the board examiner," Mary said. "Your brother is an adult. He can make holiday plans on his own." He wanted to argue that statement, but he would not ruin this day for her. Leaning over, he placed a kiss on her cheek.

"He's my little brother, dear. I will always look after him. Just as I will always be looking after our little girl here." He gently tweaked Margaret's nose.

"Yes, well, sorry to rush off, and lovely christening. Take

care of my niece until my return, won't you?" Hector backed toward the drive.

Trying one last time to extract information, Will said, "I need to know where to contact you in case of an important event."

Hector nodded, pursing his lips in that practiced wise-old-professor expression. He thought it made him look older, but it actually made him look like a boy pretending to be an adult. "Yes, yes, as soon as the itinerary is set, I will drop you a letter in the post."

"Heckie!"

The boy straightened his shoulders, looking all too much like a man. "Leave off, Will. I'm going. And I will warn you again, stop calling me by that child's name." He nodded to Mary. "Until next time." Then he turned and practically ran down the drive.

The young fool. "Damn it." When had his little brother turned into a man?

Mary placed her hand on his arm, her engraved gold wedding band glinting in the midday sun. "He will do as he wishes. You cannot force him into a mold you cast for him."

"It's a mold society cast, not me."

"Will."

"I just don't want him hurt."

"Do you want him to be miserably unhappy?"

He squeezed his lips together to keep from spouting vehement opinions—no, vehement realities—that would upset Mary, but damn the boy.

In the back of his mind, he knew who Hector would spend the fortnight with. Even if he guessed incorrectly, it was a sure bet he knew what Hector would spend his fortnight *doing.*

Through a blood red haze, Will watched the carriage

leave, glaring at the retreating dust cloud until it dissipated. What the hell was Ty doing here? He was not welcome.

He had lost the desire for making conversation and enjoying the festivities. Slamming his half-empty glass of champagne onto the tray of a passing footman, and almost toppling the man's load, he searched among the partygoers for Mary. Where the devil had she disappeared to? He stood at the edge of the crowd and stared once more at the road, fists clenched, face hurting from tightened jaws.

"Lieutenant. Oh, do excuse me, as you are no longer a lieutenant, are you? I should call you what was communicated on the invitation—the Honorable William Somerville, second son of Baron Forsythe."

Will turned and felt his face go slack for an instant before he plastered what he hoped was a congenial smile into place. "Ah, Lieutenant Baker. You could make the event." He looked to the left, just over the vile man's shoulder. He did not remember his acknowledgment of attendance. Rules dictated he would extend the invitation to officers of his old crew, but that did not mean he *expected* an appearance.

Bad blood flowed between them. Of course there would be bad blood. For twenty years, Will and Ty had been inseparable, until the incident almost two years ago. Baker was a toadying climber, always looking for the bluest blood to give him cachet. Ty's blood was bluer than the Atlantic, so Will and Baker clashed.

"Doctor, you have a beautiful family. I hope you remain as blissfully happy as you appear today."

Will was not particularly jovial at the moment. He was certain that aspect of his emotions slipped through to some extent. "Thank you, and I wish the same to you—"

"Afraid I must leave, and almost as soon as I arrived, but

please excuse me. I have a prior engagement." Baker headed off to the stables.

Will's empty platitudes wilted on his tongue and drifted away into the soft breeze, so the half-spoken words didn't actually count as a lie.

CHAPTER TWO

Hector forced himself to slow down but barely kept his steps to a walk. He was tired of Will acting as though *he* had an unblemished past, and he was frustrated by people forcing him into a convention that would never work for him. But there was one person whose nature matched his perfectly. He reached the carriage, the door held open by a footman with eyes cast down.

All he could see in the gloomy recesses were two long, elegant legs in black Hessian boots, stretching toward the door. The master of those limbs lazed back against the leather-padded walls.

Hector knew that nonchalant sprawl very well.

Intimately well.

A thrill crackled through his body at what the next two weeks would hold. Before vaulting into the beckoning darkness, he glanced over his shoulder. William stood with his feet apart as Mary took Pug from him. He glared at the coach and took a step forward, but stopped when Mary placed a hand on his arm.

Hector had known this would not be easy for Will. That was why he kept it secret for so long. That was why he hadn't revealed who he was leaving with. Bad form on his part, but he'd been protecting his holiday.

Or maybe he'd wanted to prevent trouble. Awfully noble of him. He almost chuckled, since overt flaunting was more his normal behavior than graciousness.

Noble feelings or not, he recognized that part of the thrill running through his veins was achieving something Will had not, even though he had likely been offered the chance once. The more fool him for not grasping the opportunity with both hands and holding so tight, it would never slip away.

He placed one foot on the running board of the obsidian coach, its dark recesses heralding the foray into forbidden pleasures this fortnight promised.

The vehicle lilted toward him with a creak as he stepped up, then it creaked again as it recentered when he sat across from the carriage's current occupant. The door closed, eclipsing the light. With the shades pulled low, it was difficult to see Wentworth. But Hector could picture the man in his mind. He had dreamed about that firm, elegant body every night for the past eighteen months.

If he had a talent for the brush, he could paint Wentworth from memory. The portrait would be bold, daring—ebony hair, deep sea-blue eyes, aristocratic nose, full, perfectly shaped lips above a strong chin, and straight white teeth he flashed during his rare sardonic grins. He was long, lean, powerful, and tough as spikes, though you wouldn't suspect that from such a graceful exterior. In essence, Wentworth was flawless and mature.

They shared no greeting. Hector simply absorbed Wentworth's essence, their calves touching. Thick tension filled the air, making it difficult to breathe.

The carriage jolted to a start, and as they exited the drive and joined a country lane, Wentworth opened a shade.

Golden sunlight exploded into Hector's eyes. He blinked several times and squinted before he could absorb Wentworth's beauty. The stupid grin he'd fought all day crept across his face. He should try to act aloof, sophisticated, like Wentworth, but he was just too damn happy.

"God, I thought you would never return to England." He looked out the window. "The road is empty. Seems we're the only people about. No one giving chase from the manor house." Hector launched himself onto the other man, and Wentworth made an *umpfh* before Hector kissed him. Need rushed through him at the warm brush of sinfully talented lips. The kiss lasted two quick heartbeats before strong arms pushed him back into his seat and Wentworth turned his attention to the window as he wiped a shaking hand across his mouth.

"If you are afraid of being seen, we can simply close the shade," Hector said. Then he noticed the bloody bandage on Wentworth's hand.

What a damn awkward oaf he was. Had always been, really. "You are hurt. I am so very sorry to jump on you. I probably made it worse. How were you wounded?" He would never forgive himself if he'd caused further damage.

Wentworth laughed and waved off the fussing. "Just a scratch. A stupid little incident. I should be more careful," he said in that husky baritone Hector could listen to all day.

"But I may have reinjured you."

"No, not at all."

Wentworth looked at the stained cravat, turning it one way, then the other. The loosely tied snowy bandage was red-spotted and unsightly against his pristine white cuff. "Odd thing is I feel nothing." He turned toward the window once again.

Just a scratch? He felt nothing? Then why break the kiss?

Why push him away?

Why stare out the window?

Hector swallowed. He'd thought by this time they would

be panting and straining against one another, but that had probably been too much to ask. After all, they needed some time to reacquaint themselves.

Correct?

Certainly!

Especially considering they had barely spoken ten sentences a month ago, when there'd been just enough time to pleasure each other during a chance meeting at the theater, just enough communication to rekindle their dormant lust, leave them both sticky, barely sated, and then to arrange this holiday.

Well, then, reacquaint themselves they would. "What a beautiful christening that was. I wish you could have been there. Oh, no, I suppose that wasn't possible, was it? But it was lovely, and my niece is a precious baby…Perfect day, sunshine, all the green…Won a bout at Gentleman Jackson's…Your trip to Paris…?"

Wentworth watched him with a half-smile the whole time. Hector ran out of things to say and, truly, he wanted to listen to Wentworth's arousing baritone anyway, so he added, "How are you?"

Wentworth cracked that beloved sardonic grin, and oh, the shivers it sent down his spine. "Run out of things to say already?" He laughed. "Oh, my chatty boy, I have always enjoyed your enthusiasm. Do not worry. I am well, except for this annoyance." He waved his bandaged hand. "It has been a long time since we simply conversed. I had forgotten how much you have to say."

It *had* been a long time, too long since they'd spent time together. They no longer had that easy interaction they once did. Hector could work on that, could get their affair of hearts back to the way he remembered it before the incident—steamy, intense, yet comfortable.

He grabbed Wentworth's wounded hand, kissed his wrist,

then turned and put Wentworth's arm around his shoulder as he snuggled against his firm, warm body. He held up the wounded appendage and made a vow. "I will look after this. Make sure it is well cared for." Then he put his other hand on Wentworth's thigh, slowly rubbing back and forth with a second message. *I will look after the rest of you as well.*

"In addition, I have lots of plans for us while we are in Kent."

"Do you?" Wentworth slid farther down the cushions, his legs spreading open, and fitted him snugly against his broad, strong chest. The new position allowed for better access.

Hector slid his hand up Wentworth's thigh and kept it there, letting his fingers play with Wentworth's hard muscles under smooth, cream-colored fabric.

Wentworth closed his eyes.

"Good?"

A nod.

He ran his hand farther up, reaching for a goal tucked away in wool breeches. Before he reached his target, Wentworth stopped the progression. "It will be better if we wait until reaching my estate, Sprout."

Hector hated that name. Wentworth had called him Sprout since…well, since he could remember. This, on top of Will calling him Heckie for the first time in probably a year, rubbed him the wrong way. "Perhaps you could cease using that stupid pet name."

Wentworth looked him up and down, blazing a heat trail every inch of the way. Hector nearly panted.

"You do not like the endearment I gave you when you were a boy?"

He shook his head. "I've never liked it."

"And you waited until this moment to let me know that important bit of information?"

"I've told you at least a hundred times over the past ten years, and I'm certain you remember." Hector sighed as he deduced the situation. "You are just teasing me, but do stop using that insufferable name. Makes me sound like an insignificant plant. Something, some*one* forgettable."

"Yes." The word slipped out like a lazy summer haze. "You have always felt you are forgettable, I remember. And you do not wish to be forgotten, do you?"

Of course he didn't wish to be forgotten. No one wanted to be forgotten, especially third sons. And anyway, wasn't the need to be remembered the reason for so many babies, so many wars, so many monuments? Not to mention the fact that everyone always remembered his brothers but couldn't remember *his* name. He hated being third and last born. He hated being unmemorable.

Not waiting for an answer, Wentworth continued. "If I cannot call you Sprout, then what should I call you? Hector does not roll off the tongue in a pleasant manner."

He didn't know what exactly prickled his skin, but currently he was quite annoyed. "You could call me Edmund."

"Good God, no! Edmund is more cumbersome to pronounce than your given appellation. I hate to mention this, but your family has ridiculous naming conventions."

"Ridiculous?"

"Quite so."

"But you call me Sprout."

Wentworth laughed. "Yes, but with the greatest respect."

"Arse." He nudged the other man's leg, and they both smiled. "You used to call me *dear*."

"Did I?" Wentworth said, tightening his hand on the window frame.

"You don't remember?"

"Of course, of course, *dear*."

He poked Wentworth in the ribs. "Still an arse."

"Duly noted."

They sat in silence, Hector blissfully lounging in his lover's arms. Eventually the quiet became unbearable, so he said, "Speaking of names, Wentworth is so formal. Doesn't roll of the tongue well. I can call you Tyler."

"Good God, no. I hate that name."

"How can you possibly *hate* a name?"

"I do. It means footman or tile maker or some such drivel. A layman named Tyler saved one of my ancestors, and Tyler became a cherished given name in the family after that. It is very embarrassing, really. In fact, I dislike my name so much, I never think of myself as Tyler."

"No? Then what do you think of yourself as?"

"Wentworth, of course."

Hector laughed. "You really are an arse."

Wentworth ruffled Hector's hair.

"Stop that." He tried to lean out of reach, but the carriage was too small. "I know. I'll call you Ty."

"No!" The man snorted like a bull. "No one calls me that."

"William has always called you Ty."

Wentworth's shoulders stiffened. "Not anymore." Simple words, quietly spoken. How could they convey so much pain? So much world weariness?

He reached again for the bulge at Wentworth's crotch but did not reach his goal.

Wentworth's grip, like iron manacles on his wrist, stopped him cold. "Waiting builds anticipation, increases pleasure. Be patient, Hector. Besides, this morning I have found myself in a less-than-perfect mood. Perhaps due to exhaustion. Thought I had a few more hours of energy, but apparently not. At any rate, I doubt I could pay attention if twenty-seven naked men danced around the carriage."

"You look tired. Was your journey long today?"

"Yes. I left Portsmouth at moonrise on horseback to make it back in time."

Back in time. To collect him for their holiday. Just like that, his heart swelled and his world blossomed. The most important thing at the moment was making Wentworth comfortable so he could rest.

"Here." He arranged a few cushions. "Take a respite on the way. We have a good two hours yet to go."

Wentworth settled into the plush pile and grinned. "A whole two hours. Will you not be bored?"

"Not if I have you to look forward to when we arrive."

Wentworth pulled him against his chest. "This will help me rest," he murmured.

Hector tried to sit quietly while Wentworth dozed off and on.

Occasionally, Wentworth teased his curls with long, strong fingers. It was wickedly erotic. Waiting certainly did increase the anticipation.

He had already waited eighteen months. He was long past ready, so lounging against the man he'd pined for, more like grieved for—the emotion too devastating to be anything other than grief—without gaining release was excruciating.

CHAPTER THREE

The vibrant countryside slid by the carriage windows. Bone weary but unable to sleep, Wentworth watched the perfectly straight rows of timber plantings rush past, boys fishing in a pond, then miles of green fields and sheep.

Hector's warm body nestled close, but being close to him, seeing Will again, and watching Will kiss Mary brought back vivid memories of the worst day of his life. He had hidden them so deep inside, he was disappointed to find they had not rusted and crumbled to dust.

It had happened during his last winter in Grantham, a brutally cold and windy winter season. He wanted nothing more than to sail for the Mediterranean and stay anchored at a port in Greece until his bones were thoroughly stewed.

❖

Eighteen months prior, December 18, 1806, Grantham

Waiting in a borrowed cottage far away from civilization, Wentworth looked at the overly ornate clock. It was almost midnight.

They would kill a man soon.

His turbulent emotions made him careless—or was it bolder?—than was his nature. He walked over to Hector, his lover of one spectacular month, unable to resist the boy turning into a man. His overly long, near-black hair curled in disarray, his muscular frame relaxed in a large wine-colored chair. He touched Hector's shoulder. The fabric was warm from the fire blazing in the hearth.

Hector looked so in love at that moment, you could read his emotion in the blown pupils swallowing those lovely tea-colored irises on the smooth skin of his flushed face. Wentworth, ready to explode with need, was blinded to everything around him except the lovely lad.

He never even considered the other people in the small sitting room as he allowed Hector to cover his hand with his and smile up at him.

With a roar, Will, his lifelong friend, came unhinged. "You son of a whore!" Trembling, his eyes narrowed and his breathing strident, he stared at their joined hands for a few moments, then launched himself at Wentworth, howling. "He's my little brother, you sodomizing bastard."

Wentworth blocked his blows. He wanted to reason with Will, but his own temper got the best of him. "You condescending arse...always acting so...perfect. Just because you are normal...but still you felt it your...duty to remain my friend?"

"Keep away from him, or I swear I will kill you!" Spittle flew along with the threats.

Will forced him against a recessed bookshelf. Books and wood stabbed against his spine as Will pressed one arm against his throat.

Turning to keep his windpipe from collapsing, he said, "What good would that do? He likes men. He will never find a woman to love. Never. He is unnatural just like me."

Will said nothing. Instead, he sent a short jab to Wentworth's cheek and nose.

Pain and blood clouded his vision. He no longer held his temper. He fought back. They were well matched, his height and longer reach against Will's stockier frame. They often brawled while growing up and knew each other's tactics, so no real damage was done. Because of their knowledge, most of the blows did not land.

Eventually, their fatigued muscles slowed, and they threw blows less frequently as they stumbled. They wrestled on the floor, sliding on a tasseled rug, each man trying for the upper hand. Will ended on top with arms and legs locked, and neither man could move from sheer exhaustion. Snot choked their hoarse curses.

"Will, stop it!" Mary said.

Wentworth could see Mary struggling to free herself from Hector's grip. Hector held her back, his fingers tight around her arm. Did the silly woman think she could stop them when no one could do anything to help what had been building for years? He and Will had been friends since childhood. Had fought and played and helped one another through war and Will's brutal father.

And it was this closeness that made loving Hector unforgivable. Still, Wentworth tried to make Will understand. "Let him find what happiness he can."

"With you? You traitorous bastard." Will was crimson.

"Yes, with me. I finally found someone who accepts me as I am." He bucked his hips, trying to throw Will off. "Who loves me." He glared at Will. "Let me make Hector happy."

Exhausted, they could do little more than hold each other's arms to keep any more punches from flying. Will's weight felt intimate, comforting. They could have been lovers passionately coupling, if circumstances were different.

Will's shoulders relaxed, and he sobbed into Wentworth's neck. "How could you do this? How could you? How could you?"

He felt like three kinds of ugly sea creatures for his actions, but he had always taken care of Will. He was the oldest by two years, and they were best friends, so he comforted Will. It came naturally to wrap his arms around the man.

That was when Hector yelled, "Get up, you two. Stop this. Now!"

Mary helped Will extricate himself from Wentworth's embrace, while Hector stood very still, his beautiful eyes smoldering.

Then Wentworth did the rashest thing in his whole sordid life—he decided to clear his conscience.

❖

"We will arrive at your estate soon." Hector's comment brought him out of his self-castigation.

He sat up and shook off the tension from his remembrance. "Hmm, indeed we will. I am pleased you are accompanying me. Honestly, I have found the estate dreadfully lonely since Gabriel died."

While Wentworth was away at sea, the typhus epidemic had struck. Gabriel, his favorite brother, was supposed to have inherited the title, but instead died only days before his father and the second eldest, Victor. His sister and much of the staff at Wentworth Manor followed. He did not see them nor say goodbye one last time. When he rushed home after getting word, Grandfather locked him up to keep him from going to the manor. To keep him alive. When he was the least worthy of surviving.

He stretched, as much to forget as to work out stiff

muscles, and then hugged Hector. He felt so much like Will, the man who had been by his side for nearly twenty years, through youthful friendship, through school, and through war. The brothers were almost the same size, and absolutely the same build.

Pulling Hector's cravat and collar out of the way, he nuzzled his neck.

Hector sighed and relaxed, sensual and trusting.

"I am sorry," Wentworth whispered, and Hector twisted his neck to look at him.

Turning away from Hector's eyes, he scanned the scenery. The sun, low in the sky, cast long oak shadows across grassy fields.

"Whatever for? For exhausting yourself by riding all night so you were on time to pick me up? I find that admirable."

He did not see himself as admirable. He was anything but admirable. To his ears, his apology rang hollow. Was he sorry? Sorry for hurting so many people? Sorry for the pain he had inflicted on Hector? Yes, but even more, he was sorry, deeply sorry for having lost the things that meant most in the world to him, and afraid he would lose them all over again.

❖

The carriage stopped at Hector's request, and he felt a twinge in one thigh as he climbed out of the small space. He regretted not having stopped earlier. Sitting for hours was not a favorite pastime of his. He walked to the edge of the road, loosening his tight muscles.

Wentworth exited the carriage with much more grace, and stood beside him.

Down in the valley stood Forsythe Manor. Small compared to Wentworth's estate in the neighboring valley, it was only thirty acres but nonetheless impressive in its own right. He walked down the road, knowing Wentworth and the vehicle would follow. This was his favorite part of the trip. With his family's gray stone manor in the distance, forest on one side of the road and meadow on the other, his breathing expanded and his muscles eased. This was home.

"The pond is full. Walk with me?" Hector said.

"It will be dark soon."

"Just for a moment. I've been in London too long. I need to see clean skies and clean water." They walked side by side until they reached the edge of a jade-green pond. "Look. Ducklings."

Wentworth threw his head back and laughed, startling the little downy birds.

"What the devil is so funny? You scared them away."

Wentworth ruffled his hair, and Hector leaned away and glowered at him.

"Look." Wentworth nodded toward the pond. One little duckling was out swimming around. The little bird was fast and curious, chasing an insect almost twice its size, then investigating the shore while its siblings were well hidden in the reeds. "That little fellow reminds me of you."

"What?" Hector felt his hackles rise. "I remind you of a guinea-sized baby bird? That is not quite the impression I wanted to leave you with during our fortnight together." He tossed a twig into the water.

Wentworth squeezed his shoulder. "I meant no offense. Look at the bird. What do you see?"

"A fuzzy, floating duckling."

"Yes, but look at his energy. He is constantly moving, inquisitive and inventive while his siblings hide in fear. He is an adventurer, young and strong."

Hector looked at Wentworth then. The late afternoon sun

made his skin almost glow as he watched the little bird, and at that moment, Hector felt like an adventurer. He felt brave and fearless.

"Let's go to your estate," Hector said as he stood. "There are things I want to do to you."

"With pleasure." Wentworth's smile was dark and sensuous as he ushered them to the carriage, his hand warm on the small of Hector's back.

CHAPTER FOUR

Hector removed his coat, waistcoat, and cravat and then stepped toward the large white and blue patterned bowl sitting on a chest of drawers. He dipped a linen cloth into the cool water to wash his face, wanting to be newly clean even though he'd bathed after arriving at the estate.

He'd shared a country dinner with Wentworth. Country meant the hour would be early, for there was nothing simple about the food. They dined in the manor's grand hall as spectacularly as any king, at a long table lit by candles set into silver candlesticks. They enjoyed tender pheasant stuffed with truffles and turnips, fluffy hot bread, buttered carrots, and fresh berries with cream. Hector had eaten his fill, pushed his heavy chair back, and then taken brandy.

Neither of them lingered over the drink.

Ready to get on with the more energetic parts of the evening, Hector excused himself and went to his room. He'd been to the manor many times as a child, so the opulent carpets, flooring, and paneling held no interest for him. He was much more preoccupied with preparing himself for a visit from Wentworth.

He was reaching for a nightshirt when the knock he anticipated sounded on his door. He smiled. At dinner, Wentworth had hinted he would call that evening.

Walking to the door, he pulled on the shirt, wishing he'd skipped the brandy. He felt slow and drowsy, not at all the way he wanted to welcome his very good friend into bed after such a long absence.

Wentworth sauntered in, aloof and godlike, his ebony hair glinting in the light of the lone candle by Hector's bed.

Lethargy forgotten, he reached for Wentworth, who avoided his touch, gripped his shoulder, and pushed him face against the door. Hot breath excited the skin at the back of his neck.

"Do you know what I have missed most about fornicating with you, Hector?"

He shook his head, forehead rubbing against freshly polished wood.

"I missed those sweet, smooth thighs."

At the reminder of what was once one of their favorite activities, Hector's cock grew hard and needy in his trousers. He grabbed the doorframe with both hands, one on each side of the door, and spread his feet a foot apart. "Slip my pants down. I need to feel you rubbing against my balls, my hole."

The breath at the back of his neck hitched, but sure fingers undid his falls and cool air soon tickled the back of his arse.

A firm hand slid up the inside of one thigh. "So smooth, just as I remembered. No hair here, perfect for a man's prick."

Hector shivered and pushed back against the strong, large body behind him. Felt the hard cock behind cloth so fine, it felt like a layer of cream between himself and what he wanted sliding between his legs.

"Did you bring oil?"

He felt Wentworth nod along the top of his head.

He placed his feet together. "Use it." He heard the pop of the stopper and then felt a hard, warm poke between his legs.

He looked down to see the dark-pink head of Wentworth's impressive cock slip between his thighs, and then felt Wentworth's oiled hand on his greedy flesh.

"Feels so good. So firm and smooth."

Hector pushed back to allow for more friction on his balls and perineum, the pressure right under his cock so close to his hole. It was an exquisite accompaniment to the slip and slide on his aching prick. God, he would come in a few more strokes.

He turned his head to kiss Wentworth, but the angle would not allow for such intimacies. He could only see a strained, almost pained profile. And then he came. Huge contractions expelled seed out of him in rhythmic spurts as he rocked himself into Wentworth's fist. Closing his eyes, he rode the tingles and rush of euphoria until drained.

Sometime during his climax, Wentworth came as well. Two long, pearly streaks of seed dripped down the dark oak door.

Hector's knees nearly collapsed as he said, "Bed."

They stumbled toward the firm cotton mattress together. Slumberous and sated and feeling the effects of the encounter and the brandy, he mumbled, "Come to bed with me, Wentworth." He slipped in, holding up one side of the blanket in invitation. He felt the bed dip but was nearly asleep before his head hit the pillow.

When the rising sunlight filtered through a gap in the drawn curtains, Hector woke alone.

❖

Four days of fucking, drinking, and excellent company had Wentworth up early every morning looking forward to the day. He would open and read the prior day's correspondence. Invitations, he ignored; a letter from an impoverished third cousin asking for funds, he could postpone answering; and the notice from his solicitor about a property he wished to purchase could wait as well. The owner still did not wish to sell. Nothing urgent. Nothing from his commodore. Nothing from his second-in-command. So each day there were no distractions from enjoying time with his guest.

After a good day hiking his estate they were having dinner, and he found himself laughing at Hector's stories.

"You cannot be serious."

Hector smiled. "One hundred percent earnest. I swear to you I added no embellishment."

He chuckled. "I can envision old Professor Weatherston standing to his full height of exceptionally short, grabbing— what was the boy's name?"

"Timothy Blair," Hector said, his voice quivering with mirth.

"Right. Grabbing young Blair by the ear and marching him out of the classroom, dripping lemon curd with each step." He laughed. In fact, he had been laughing all day. Hector knew how to tell a good story, and the effect had Wentworth's face muscles hurting from overuse.

"Tell me again how Blair managed to obtain a bucketful of curd."

"Well, it turned out his mother—"

The dining room door opened, and Wentworth frowned as his butler approached, carrying the ever-present silver salver. His joy collapsed. He knew with a gut-gnawing surety Will was calling, even if Wentworth did not fully understand why he was here.

"You have a visitor, my lord."

He took the calling card presented on the salver, and his blood ran cold at the touch of smooth cream paper. He shoved the card deep into one pocket.

"At six in the evening? That is rather unconventional," Hector said.

Something must have shown on his face, or more likely Hector noticed him stiffen, for he said, "Wentworth, is something amiss?"

"No. No, just...an acquaintance. I will inquire about his purpose for the visit and send him on his way. Then we can have a port or brandy."

Hector smiled at that statement, and Wentworth left to confront Will.

He went to the drawing room, wondering how his numb limbs managed to take him down two hallways and a flight of stairs. Seizing a deep breath before opening the door, he readied himself and then entered with all the aristocratic arrogance he could muster.

William Somerville stood at ease, his expression blank, but Wentworth was not fooled. He knew there was a lit fuse under the surface.

"I hope you do not intend to stay overly long. I have a very pleasant guest I *desire* to return to." He was not certain why he chose such inflammatory words to greet Will. But after two years of silence...

His words had a predicable outcome. Will tightened his jaws and curled his upper lip. "I am fully aware of your guest, and that is why I'm here."

He approached Will, who stood tall and proud, just as handsome as he remembered. "Brandy?"

"No."

"How have you been? Forgive me, but I forgot to ask the

past several years in which you have not spoken to me." He wanted to say the words sarcastically, but their decades-long friendship neutralized them.

"You mean other than worrying about my little brother, who has a sodomite chasing his tail?" He stepped closer to Wentworth and whispered, "How is he, Ty?"

He could see Will's chest rise and fall rapidly. He assumed the quick breathing was out of anger, but at one time that physical response had been elicited by desire.

Just that thought alone had his prick quickening. Damn fickle organ.

He tried to step away from temptation, but his feet were cemented to the floor. "He is well. Enjoying his holiday with me."

Will left a gentle caress along Wentworth's stubbled chin with one strong, calloused finger.

Wentworth closed his eyes and clung to the lingering sensation of that touch, remembering a simpler time. Forcing himself to speak, he said, "Your brother is no longer a boy. He has the right to make his own choices."

"But, Ty, does he have all the information he needs to make the best decision on who he spends time with?"

His eyes snapped open in time to see Will's scowl turn into a sour apricot smile. Wentworth moved back a few inches. Will had been as close as a lover preparing for a kiss, and as angry as a viper whose nest was raided by a badger. He could not help the shiver that racked his body. For a few moments he'd been ready to close the distance between them as if their past had never turned bitter. Stepping away was the only way to clear his head.

He walked to the brandy decanter, poured two glasses, and set one down. "It is here if you want it." He went to the settee and rested his arse on the back. "Let me ask you the same question. Did Mary have all the information she needed to make a decision when she agreed to wed you?"

"Yes, actually. I told her the night of the fight, and she had three months to change her mind if it worried her."

Wentworth whistled. "My, but I would have loved to have been a portrait on the wall that night."

"Afraid you would have been disappointed. Mary is very practical. She asked a few questions and then proclaimed she was relieved I didn't have any female ex-lovers who were still my friends."

Wentworth was rather taken aback by that. A more likely reaction would be gnashing of teeth and tearing of flesh.

"So, I surmise from your evasion of my question that you have not told Hector about *us*." The last word was a lover's murmur.

Damn, what was Will's game? Well, whatever his intent, it was making Wentworth feel like a cad. And when he felt worthless, he struck out.

"Yes, well, there is no reason to tell him. As you know, the two of us will never be an *us* again." He downed his brandy, enjoying the burn. When he walked to the door, he did not feel completely steady on his feet. "I will have a footman show you out."

"Ty. I am staying at Stephen's estate for a day or two. Come for a visit. We need to…*talk*."

Wentworth stood with his hand on the door latch, familiar feelings and physical sensations destroying his ability to think. Eventually, he simply left the room.

❖

That night, as Wentworth stumbled to Hector's room, carrying a bottle of superlative brandy and a wagonload of apprehension, he worried over what Will was offering. It had been so long since Will left him, he had trouble believing this visit was only about issuing a proposition. So why did his body and soul feel like that was exactly what his ex-lover had proposed?

Certainly, Will had not tired of his wife. He had been smitten just a few months prior. Could someone fall out of love so quickly? Or was it just that Will missed male affection? If so, why not stray before now? Did Will miss him, his closest friend from childhood, his first lover?

He stopped in his tracks. Would he take Will back? The man he pined for, mourned the loss of for what seemed like centuries?

Was sex even on offer?

If he went to see Will, would he be met with a group of burly footmen and a well-deserved beating? He sighed and rolled his shoulders to lessen the tension gathering there.

God, but his head spun from too much brandy and too many unanswered questions. Perhaps he would simply go to Will and ask his real intentions so he could lift this unease off his shoulders.

He stopped at Hector's door, which opened immediately.

"I thought you would never arrive. In here. Now!" The boy grabbed him by the dressing gown collar and yanked him inside.

Laughing, he stumbled forward. "Eager, are you?"

"Yes."

He barely had time to place the brandy on a table before Hector forced their lips together and wrestled them onto the bed with a big flop that made them bounce and that set them off laughing. Minutes later, Hector sat up and reached for his head. "Oh, perhaps I had a dram too much port after dinner. My head is just a smidgen…um…muzzy."

"Muzzy?"

"Indeed."

"Too much sugar in port. You need to cut it with something. I have just the thing."

"What is that?"

"Brandy, of course." He rearranged the pillows, propped himself against the headboard, and beckoned Hector to do the same as he reached for the bottle.

"I'm not at all certain that is a sound idea."

"Of course it is." He managed the cork with some effort and took a mouthful directly from the bottle. The vintage was so smooth, it did not burn going down. "Have a little. You will soon start to feel better."

Hector looked uncertain as he took a drink, then another. "Mmm, that is good."

He laid one arm over the young man's sturdy shoulders and took another drink himself. "Feeling better?"

"Actually, yes. Quite a fast remedy for drinking too much port. May I have more?"

They passed the bottle back and forth a few times as he unfastened Hector's velvet-lined, blue silk gown. And then no other clothes kept him from touching Hector's fine skin.

Humming his pleasure, Hector slid farther down the bed and tried to pull him along as well.

Wentworth took one more sip and then offered the bottle to the beautiful young man lying prone before him. Hector drank as Wentworth opened his own robe, the tie scarlet red. He chuckled. "This reminds me of the time I stole a red curtain rope and tried to lower myself from my bedroom balcony to an oak branch many feet below."

"Did you make it to the oak?"

"Not at all. In fact, I hung there screaming for help until a maid rushed in and pulled me up. I thought I would fall to my death."

Hector snorted.

"You laugh, but imagine my humiliation when grandfather found out I had to be saved by a female, and one in service no less." They both laughed, and Hector shared an embarrassing story as Wentworth pulled their bodies close and wrapped them both in their robes, warm skin to warm skin. The position was more comforting than arousing, especially as fatigue and a chill started to set into his frame.

As they shared stories and laughed more than he could remember having done in years, Hector found Wentworth's cock and went to work with an uncoordinated effort that had them both near choking on their mirth.

"My dear, I'm afraid the heart is willing and all, but..."

"I believe the brandy was not such a grand idea after all, Wentworth. My head is spinning." He giggled.

"You must be in your cups, if you resort to giggling like a girl." That sent him to giggling as well, and soon they pulled up the bed covers and tittered until they were too exhausted to stay awake.

❖

Wentworth slept so late, he would have to sneak into his own room while the servants prowled the living quarters. He slid out of bed and attempted to tie his robe, but a patch of cool air on his right thigh suggested he'd made a hash of that simple task. He grabbed the brandy bottle—there were still a few dregs—and left his rumple-haired lover softly snoring in bed.

He snagged his toe on the hall runner, catching himself

awkwardly on the wall before he fell. Shaking his head, he realized his thoughts were still bleary. *Damnation, still foxed.* Shaking his head again to clear away the fog, he stumbled to his chambers and poured himself the rest of the brandy. Might as well be civilized this early in the morning and drink from a glass.

He would figure out later what to do about the shambles of his life. Currently all he wanted to do was finish his drink, crawl into bed, and forget about everything in the oblivion of sleep.

CHAPTER FIVE

Wentworth poured himself another brandy and slid down into his large, plush study chair, legs stretching toward the brass guard of the fireplace. It was the warmest spot in the drafty old manor and his favorite brandy. Today, he needed both.

He'd sent Hector off on some fool's errand just to get rid of him. What a stupid idea, bringing the boy here. He should have known Will could not leave well enough alone. Hell, he should have stayed in France, but his cock had done the thinking at the time.

Now he was having second thoughts and needed time to think. To decide what to do. What to tell Hector, because it was a bloody certainty that Will would tell him everything once this fortnight was over.

Sating his lust on William's brother...No, it was more than that. Much more. But he had done so many things to be angry with himself about. It was easiest to concentrate on only one for now. He could castigate himself for the others later.

Fucking Hector was not revenge, but Will would certainly think so.

He did not start the liaison with Hector to punish Will, but the attraction to this boy—was it only due to a resemblance to someone he'd at one time longed to have above all else? He'd never been able to answer that question, and his uncertainty and past actions disgusted him.

For the love of Christ, he'd slept with both brothers, and Hector did not know.

He stood and paced the room, heels resounding on the oak floor. "Damn it all to hell." He kicked the marble fireplace surround. His boot left a long scuffmark on the white and green stone.

What was he doing, meddling with somebody's life? A vibrant, charismatic youth's life? All this just to…To what? To decide if what they had before was real? If these new remembrances slowly creeping into his emotionally sluggish brain were true or simply a shadow of what he'd once wanted?

The past week had been bright conversations and moments of extraordinary passion, sometimes almost beastly copulation, with only a hint of culpability. And now, after Will's visit, he suddenly felt surrounded by hours and hours that passed like weeks. Hours of guilt, shame, mental self-flagellation, and fear.

He didn't necessarily consider himself a good man, but he certainly did not make a habit of constant deceit that rose to the level of betrayal. Trying to remember his many lies of omission, keeping up with the heavy energy of deception while entertaining someone as lively as Hector, was near impossible.

He took a sip of oaky liquid. The liquor slid down his throat, smooth as fresh spring water. The lack of burn meant he was already drunk. He took another sip.

"For God's every loving blasphemy, Gabriel, what would you do?" He glared at the portrait of his older brother, the Wentworth heir, dead these past seven years. "Nothing to say? Yes, well, you were not very helpful in these matters before, so I am not surprised." He raised his glass to the portrait of a tall, lean, dark-haired young man of whom Wentworth was starting to lose memory. Quiet and studious, Gabriel would have made a much better viscount than the current sham. "I will have to make my own decisions, then. Not that I have a tried and true record for this sort of thing."

Best to send Hector home, where his family could take care of his soon-to-be-broken heart. What would he tell the boy? Not the truth, certainly. The truth would be too painful for everyone. So what would be his excuse?

Hell, was Hector really only two-and-twenty? God, it should be a crime what he did with that boy's body. He laughed, the sound like cannon blasts in the quiet room. What was he thinking? It *was* a crime. Screwing the lad the way he did was sodomy.

He, an officer in His Majesty's Royal Navy, committing a hangable offense on a man barely out of school.

He laughed again, the sound dark and flat.

What he really wanted was to enjoy Hector's fine body until they were both too exhausted to move or even think, for that matter. Except after Will had reminded him he was scum, thoughts of screwing Hector instigated maudlin judgments about his deception. He leaned a forearm on the chimneypiece, contemplating the charred bricks surrounding the fire.

He closed his eyes, unwanted memories pouring into his mind.

A sunny day. A christening. A beautiful, happy family. A precious bundle of joy. Then there was William, handsome, perfect William, glowing with an ecstasy for life. Glowing with love. Glowing with all these wonderful, lovely things Wentworth would never be part of because he'd cheated a friend.

He flung his glass into the fireplace. It shattered, some of the glass flying out and tinkling on the hardwood floor. The shards of crystal crunched under his boots as he staggered to the sideboard for another glass and a splash of brandy. He took the amber liquid back to his chair.

"Bloody brilliant, Wentworth. Damned bloody brilliant bastard you are. What do you have planned next? Flinging not-quite-innocent young men off the ramparts?"

God, his thinking was muddled from the drink. Not that his thinking was sound these past few years even without spirits, but this morning…

Approaching footsteps sounded staccato-like on the parquet teak floor outside his study. The door burst open, and he turned to bark at the intruder but stopped the retort before he shriveled a young man's enthusiasm. At least, before he could shrivel Hector's self-esteem beyond what he had these past two years.

"Wentworth," Hector called jovially, carrying a silver tray full of fresh treats and a newspaper stuffed under one arm. "I have the *Times* for you. I would wager you didn't think I could find one and return so soon." He closed the door with a heel. "Turns out Stephen's subscription has not yet been transferred to London."

For a moment his heart stopped, then beat double-time. Hector might have met Will at their brother's home, but if that had been the case, the boy would no longer be flirtatious.

"I also stopped by the kitchen and brought some delicacies I'm certain must be your favorites, since cook nearly forced me to take one of each. Damn, but you do have fast horses." He lowered his voice and switched topics once again, sending Wentworth's inebriated brain swirling. "I plan to feed these treats to you, piece by piece, with my own hands." Hector laughed, free and radiant, his cheeks pink from sunshine and his hair ruffled from fresh air. He wore a rather flattering forest green riding suit that highlighted his sun-tinted skin and dark eyes.

How could anyone be so luminous after Wentworth's mismanagement of their affair, after he had overnight turned into such a moody bastard? "Oh," he said, trying to sound intrigued, but instead, the word held the enthusiasm of a well-used whore on her eighth tup of the day.

Undaunted, the boy placed the silver salver on an empty chair and knelt in front of him, shimmying his way between his legs, crowding his intimate space. His *very* intimate, brandy-dampened space.

He looked to the door. The boy had let loose of his senses, forgetting to throw the latch.

"I brought strawberry tarts, spotted dick, and berry trifle sweetened with honey. One of them surely is your favorite. All of them are some of my preferred confections." He pointed to the tray. "Which do you want me to lick off your chest, arms, thighs…?" His enticing finger burned a trail of desire from his chest to the fastening of his trousers.

Hector looked up with big, happy eyes. They were the most unusual shade, like sun shining through a crystal decanter full of fresh, strong tea. They almost glowed when not shadowed by those sinfully long eyelashes.

God, the lad was beautiful. Wentworth's cock stirred even through the haze of brandy.

The past week they had fucked as regularly as dining, and that's all it was, fucking. Sex. Nothing softer. Nothing gentler. Not lovemaking. It was *not* lovemaking.

He could not make love to someone he'd lied to every time they had come together. He could not waste that emotion for a second time on someone who would leave as soon as he learned the truth.

"So, I thought I would take a bite of this tart." Hector

chewed the bite and swallowed. "And let you taste it on me." He pulled himself up by the chair arms and leaned in for a kiss.

Desire shot through Wentworth's body to his cock as he watched Hector lick his lips, and he wanted nothing more than to run his tongue across that perfect mouth. He leaned in and touched those flawless lips. He inhaled and smelled springtime. The scent had his alcohol-muddled brain obsessing on thoughts of guilt, sending desperation racing through his brain and blood at nauseating speed. He slammed against the headrest and turned his head.

He had to stop this. He needed time to think. Unfortunately, all his slow brain could conjure was hurtful nonsense. "Stop. I prefer my food whole and on a plate. Plus, what kind of idiot does not take the time to lock a door when planning an act of perversion?"

Hector pulled back as if struck, his eyes wide. A muscle jerked near the right side of his mouth.

Damnation. He did not want to hurt the boy. He really did not. Then why had he brought him here, knowing full well Hector was smitten? He should have realized this situation would be rough waters to navigate, and he not up to the task.

"Here, get up off your knees. Sit over there. I will eat my tart, you can eat yours, and then we will discuss what to do with the rest of the day."

Sitting across from each other, they ate in silence, the confections nothing more than hardtack in his mouth.

With one eyebrow raised, Hector looked at the shimmering shards of glass on the hardwood floor near the fireplace, looked at him, then looked away, obviously thinking about chastising him for drinking in the morning. Or more likely thinking of asking why he was such an ill-tempered bastard.

Instead, the tactful young man said, "I have a thought. It would be pleasant if we went for a ride this afternoon. Race around the opens. Test the speed on some of the other horses you have in your stables."

Actually, that was a smashing idea. If he had not woken drunk and continued drinking until he was three sheets to the wind already at...He looked at the clock, but the hands refused to stay still on any one number. If he were not drunk already this morning, he would enjoy a bruising ride.

"I thought I might take the day to see to personal matters, correspondence and the like." He motioned toward a writing table, its inlaid top covered with papers and sealed letters. Turning back to Hector, he added, "Perhaps catch up on the sleep you have stolen from me the past handful of nights."

The boy looked right, then left, but nodded with a weak smile.

"Come now, you have to give an old seaman time to recuperate. After all, I am not used to keeping these types of hours. Unless there is a war on, of course."

Hector's natural enthusiasm reasserted itself. "How about I keep you company while you work? I can even help. My professors always said I am a genius with numbers."

"Indeed? I would love a demonstration someday, but not this one. I would get nothing done at all with you in the room."

"But...I don't understand." Hector sighed, shoulders slouching.

Here it comes. Maybe getting the confrontation over with, allaying his guilt early, was what he really wanted anyway. After all, he should have told Hector two years ago.

"Why did you ask me here? I seem to be a bother to you today."

Wentworth took a deep breath, picked up the brandy glass he couldn't remember placing on the empty chair by the pastry tray, and downed it in one satisfying gulp. He then looked at Hector.

What could he say to that? He wasn't completely sure of the answer, so he spouted off some nonsense to buy himself time to think. "I asked you here because you tricked me, made me agree when I was only one stroke away from reaching my climax."

Hector smiled at that truth.

"I will admit, a holiday full of sex was not terribly difficult to convince me to agree to, of course. You do enjoy the intimacies, do you not?" Wentworth rubbed the front of his trousers in an uncharacteristically vulgar fashion, trying to put distance between him and the boy. In for a shilling... "From all outward appearances, you do enjoy fornicating."

"Is that the *only* reason you asked me here?"

There was the rub. He, Viscount Wentworth, captain of the HBMS *Dragon*, always knew what he was about, never dithered over an action or a decision. However, this situation and this slip of a boy jumbled his thinking.

Hector's handsome face hardened. "Before you left the country, before...Grantham, I thought it was more than sex. I thought you cared for me. You said as much at the time."

Had he? He did not wholly recall. That time of his life, the worst time of his existence, was now only a handful of blurry, painful memories. Memories that were slowly, agonizingly, resurfacing and sneaking back into his sleeping and waking mind.

The silence went on far too long before Hector continued, "Well then, good to know where I stand. I'm a diversion during your two weeks in the country, while you take care of affairs. I'm here to keep your dick oiled and your arrogance stroked."

He perked one infernal eyebrow over a tea brown eye, the act so much like his brother's.

Good God, everything about Hector reminded him of William, of his guilt.

His presence reminded him of bad decisions concerning Hector and Lieutenant—now Doctor—William Somerville, self-proclaimed research physician, who had served under Wentworth for thirteen years.

His best friend. The man he had always loved. Would always love in some fashion.

The man he had worshipped for twenty goddamn bloody years and then betrayed. After deceiving Will, how could he countenance loving another? He was not good enough for any man.

He clutched the empty glass and, after two tries, stood.

Hector also stood, his stance stiff and straight. "I'm sorry. Well…Damn. No, I'm not sorry. I have been nothing if not a good guest. Therefore, I will not apologize for anything. If you want me to leave, I will." The boy stood facing him with the courage of a tiger. It was a good look on him.

Did he want the boy to go? Wentworth walked to the window, unable to hold Hector's steady brown gaze. He parted the curtains and looked out through distorted glass. The day was beautiful and sunny. He should be out riding, this boy beside him. Instead, he picked up the decanter and poured another glass, trying to incinerate the loathsome feeling in his gut.

Hector came up beside him and touched his shoulder. "Please, tell me what is wrong. I…I know I talk too much. Especially when I'm nervous."

Heat from Hector's grasp seeped through the superfine cloth. A strange churning in his stomach had him worrying he might lose all the fine brandy he had enjoyed.

"I am a good listener. Tell me if you will, and I can help you through your turmoil." He ran his fingers along the fine hairs at Wentworth's neck.

He closed his eyes. His heart flipped, then flipped again as if turning somersaults in his chest. The touch felt so good, so damned good.

The past week with the boy had been stimulating, but every time he smelled Hector or kissed him, the flavor reminded him of William.

Reminded him of his guilt, of his treachery. Reminded him of rejection.

You are a sad case, Wentworth. It was so long ago, and it would never happen again. The man he loved back then was no longer; the man he dreamed about every night for years had refused him, had broken his heart, and was now married with a baby girl. Despite Wentworth's duplicity, Will had formed a normal, happy life. The knowledge of what he did to wreck that happiness crushed him day by day, hour by hour, grinding him to dust. It did not matter if most of the skullduggery happened before he and Hector came together the first time around.

He squeezed Hector's hand, then walked back to the plush chair but did not sit. "I am just in the blue doldrums. I will be fine tomorrow."

Hector did not turn from the window. "How is your wound?"

"Fine." He raised the hand and wiggled his fingers, studying the scab across the thick part of his thumb. "Go enjoy the sun. I will entertain you tomorrow."

"All right, then, but if you are *not* better tomorrow, I'm sending for a doctor." Hector walked over stiffly. Standing toe to toe, he smoothed the hair off Wentworth's forehead.

He closed his eyes and enjoyed the light caress, then

opened his eyes, and there was Hector, a gorgeous man in his own right. A man too good for him.

Grabbing Hector's hand, he kissed his long, elegant fingers. "Tomorrow."

Hector nodded, gave him a brilliant smile that showed perfect white teeth, and left him alone with his thoughts.

Alone with his regrets.

CHAPTER SIX

The next day dawned bright and beautiful with the occasional white cloud drifting slowly across a deep blue sky. Hector resolved not to let Wentworth waste the rare sunshine like he had yesterday by sitting in his study, curtains drawn, drinking himself into a stupor. The weather was too perfect, and one week of his fortnight with the handsome viscount had already come and gone. He would not waste any more time.

That was what led to them trotting down a narrow country lane atop prime horseflesh.

Wentworth guided a very large gray mare. The horse was strong and bold like her rider. With shining ebony hair tousled by the breeze, he was so handsome, it almost hurt to look at him. Gone were the pinched lines of tension around his mouth and eyes, but Hector wanted more. He wanted to see the man smile.

So he put on his most innocent expression and offered a challenge. "Such a beautiful stretch of road, why don't we—"

Apparently, he had tried his innocent guise too many times because Wentworth immediately leaned over the mare's neck and spurred her on. Ready for an excuse to run, she launched forward, her first step a bounding leap.

It took a few seconds to spur his horse into action, and

seconds equaled five horse lengths. Hector would never catch up, but he didn't mind having the chance to watch Wentworth, an excellent horseman. Actually, he was excellent at everything. The man emanated grace, power, elegance.

The long-backed bay gelding between his legs gathered and lengthened. Hector had chosen the horse because he looked bred for speed—long, lean, and twitchy. And damn, the horse was fast. They were gradually closing the distance to the gray mare but would arrive at a fork in the lane about a half mile ahead before catching her, unless he coaxed more speed out of the gelding. He kicked its flanks and felt a slight shift in gait, a sudden surge of power, and then the race was truly on.

He gained another length, and then another and another. The horses now galloped side by side. Wentworth glanced over, and his eyebrows shot up. Aha! He had not expected to be bested. Especially after rushing the start before the challenge had been issued.

Hector laughed, and the wind filled his lungs. He closed his mouth to the sudden rush of air and concentrated on the speed and his horse. They reached the fork in the road less than a foot before Wentworth's beast.

He reined in, hooting in triumph, and then turned. The two horses circled each other, their satisfaction showing in high, swishing tails and bobbing heads. He and Wentworth stared at one another, breathing fast and deep as if they had just finished a rousing romp in bed. Hector's heart pounded. Lust rushed through his veins.

Wentworth gave him a slanted smile.

At last. The race had been a good idea.

Hector laughed. "You cheated, my lord."

"There was no cheating involved. I simply maximized my chances by anticipating your actions. Besides, I had to take the advantage. You picked the best horse in my stables." A mere whisper of a smile played over his sensuous lips, and Wentworth went from sinfully handsome to young and carefree. In a word—well, two words, because one word simply was not enough to describe his lover—wickedly gorgeous.

Hector, needing a distraction to get his lust under control, patted the gelding's sleek brown neck and looked at him with pride. The horse snorted, likely commenting on his exemplary performance. "He is probably the best horse in this county, Wentworth. Prime horseflesh. His stride is long and strong as if he were born to race."

"Indeed he was."

"Really?"

"Hmm. His sister did a stint at the courses in Ascot. Went lame and never proved herself, but I think she could have done so, judging by this big fellow." He reached over and patted the horse. "Has speed, stamina, and heart."

Horses side by side, nose to tail, his knee only inches from his heart's wish, Hector took one step toward claiming his desire. Laying a hand on Wentworth's thigh, he felt the tight muscles under cream-colored wool, then leaned closer.

Wentworth leaned away, looked down at their contact, his breath labored, pupils dilated. He ever so slowly released one rein and placed his hand over Hector's. He squeezed and closed his eyes.

The warmth he felt through two layers of kidskin must have been imagined, but it slipped all the damn way down to his cock. He wanted, needed, to catch Wentworth's gaze, but he looked around and then released Hector's hand, leaving an ache where moments ago lay contentment.

Wentworth nodded in the direction they traveled. "Come, we need to walk the horses."

Head still hazy with lust and disappointment at the loss of contact, he turned his mount and lined up alongside the other. They walked the horses for about a half mile in silence, swaying slightly in their saddles. Eventually, Wentworth veered the mare onto a weedy trail.

Always one for adventure, Hector followed, his curiosity piqued. Where were they going?

They arrived at a small grassy clearing. Wentworth stopped and dismounted into lush, calf-high grass.

Hector followed suit, and after letting the horses have a drink, they tethered them to a tree. He stretched, first one side, then the other. It felt good to ride, to feel as if he were flying across the countryside. But he was always glad to get his feet back on solid ground again in control of his motions.

He saw Wentworth looking at him as he twisted out a kink in his side. The man did not smile. In fact, he did not move. Just stared. But when Hector twisted back, Wentworth was headed toward a stream. He knelt and took a sip. "Mmm. Try this. It is the sweetest water in the surrounding five counties."

Dry as a sunbaked trout, Hector squatted and drank. "The water is good. Spring fed?" He wiped the drips of cool water from his chin with his sleeve.

"Yes." Wentworth leaned back on both elbows in the grass, staring at him, one leg crooked up.

Never had Hector seen a more inviting pose, and he was smart enough to seize the opportunity. He crawled the two feet between them and then crept up one muscular thigh as Wentworth lowered his other leg, sat up, and reached out to Hector.

The feeling of Wentworth's seaman-roughened hands, strong, warm on his cheek, one thumb rubbing across his upper lip, was carnal heaven. He wanted to close his eyes so the only sensation was the caress, but he'd been starving for this intimacy too long. He would not deprive himself of any vision of his lover. Remembering the irresistible flavor of

Wentworth's kisses, he longed to taste his uniqueness again. But he had not deeply tasted him for what felt like days.

For some obscure reason, aside from a peck or two, Wentworth had not yet returned his kiss since yesterday, when he was deep in his cups. Their reunion trip should be full of kisses, and now was the time. He would wait no longer.

Wentworth leaned back into the grass and gently pushed Hector's head toward his crotch. His disappointment lasted but a trice. Right under his nose stood a raging cock straining against the cream-colored fabric.

He sat back on his heels and made quick work of opening Wentworth's breeches. That glorious cock, so big, so thick, with one vein running up along the underside, bounced up at him, inviting, standing proud from a bush of glossy ebony hair. He laid his head on Wentworth's thigh and stroked his lower abdomen. Lazing there a moment, he just breathed him in. Musky male and wool. *Mmm.*

His own cock strained against his trouser flaps, so hard it hurt. Ready for this, needing this, he rubbed his nose in the crook of the other man's thigh and breathed deeply.

Wentworth moaned.

He licked one ball, running his tongue around it, then the other, relishing the faint, salty taste.

Wentworth grabbed Hector's hair in his fist, pulling until it tugged at the roots.

Moving his lips slowly up the engorged member, he worshipped and caressed that blue vein all the way up, relishing the sparkling, briny dew at the tip. Then he swallowed his cock in a long, slow glide.

Wentworth hitched up and shoved Hector's head down, almost gagging him before Hector relaxed and enjoyed the hard knock at the back of his throat. Once, twice, three times. Then Hector slowed. He did not want Wentworth to come this way.

He teased his cock for several minutes, making Wentworth squirm before releasing him. No need for anyone to come yet.

"I need...Hector, I want you. *Now.*"

He only smiled at the demand.

"Do something, damn the world to hell, before I combust."

He laughed and reached into his coat pocket. He'd prepared for any and all possibilities since setting out on this holiday, and what he wanted now was to be fucked senseless. Penetrated by the man he'd worshipped for more than a decade and had loved since the birthday he turned twelve, and Wentworth, newly home from sea, looked so important and invincible in his blue uniform.

Now no longer a lad, Hector was a man with adult needs, who wanted to be fucked by Wentworth more than he wanted air. He handed off the jar of unguent and removed the trousers he'd donned instead of breeches just for such hoped-for activities.

Positioning himself above his lover, Hector almost laughed at Wentworth, who stared at the jar, mouth partially open.

"Hector?"

❖

The exhilaration from the bruising ride had gone to his head. Wentworth swore the whole experience—trees, sky, Hector—wrapped him in an almost opium-like euphoria.

"I want you to fuck me, Wentworth. Prepare me." An expression similar to a zealot's lit Hector's face—lips parted, nostrils flared, eyes half-lidded, face flushed. Breathtaking.

What a heady feeling, knowing Hector wanted him so completely. He fumbled for the jar, dropped it, then picked it up again with a handful of grass, but he scooped out a large dollop without vegetation. The thick cream, warm from Hector's body, issued the scent of roses. He slicked his penis, then had to squeeze the base to control his rush toward ecstasy.

Taking a deep breath, he slowly slid one finger behind Hector's balls, found the opening, and rimmed the puckered muscle slowly, circling and circling.

That caress alone almost set Wentworth off. His cock leaked in anticipation of sliding into that sweet hole. His own arse puckered with want. He slipped one finger in, then two.

Hector took them without complaint, his lithe, young body writhing. Wentworth knew from Hector's improved knowledge and sexual assertiveness that the lad had taken lovers in the time they were apart, but Wentworth had not asked anything about these men. He did not want to think about them.

Scissoring his fingers, Wentworth opened the hole enough to slip in a third. His cock jumped at the tightness and warmth. He would take Hector, soon. Very soon.

Hector gritted his teeth and looked at the sky, seeming to fight for control. A thin layer of sweat coated his face.

Three fingers moved slowly in and out without resistance now, so he crooked them forward to find that spot.

"No," Hector yelled, nearly crumpling atop him.

"Did I hurt you?"

"Stop, just stop. I'm going to…" He clenched around the still fingers. "Stop for a second. I want you inside me when I come." Shaking and breathing heavily, he pushed Wentworth's fingers out and scooted up. Aligning cock to hole, he sat slowly on Wentworth's achingly hard staff. Inch by excruciatingly slow inch, Hector slid down.

Wentworth wanted to drive up into that blissful channel, almost mad with want. It took all his control not to force his way. Finally, oh so late in arriving, Wentworth was inside Hector's sweet, sweet grip.

The pressure along his shaft was almost unbearable. Too intense. Too exquisite. He would not last, and he had to give Hector an orgasm first. As much of a bounder as he'd been yesterday, he could at least hold back his pleasure until he made Hector come. He owed him that much. He began to rock, slowly, aiming his prick to the sensitive spot deep inside him.

Hector, head back, eyes closed and mouth open, moaned. The sound was low, primal, erotic as hell.

This would be a fast coupling, Wentworth knew. It would be near impossible for either one of them to hold back. Not with the spiraling edge of an orgasm already tickling the back of his spine. He quickened his lunges, which began to keep pace with his breath. Up. Down.

Grabbing Hector's hips, he thrust into him, hard, lifting him. Together they found an age-old rhythm, older than the hills themselves.

❖

He loved Wentworth, had loved him for so many years, worshipped him since almost the first moment they'd met. As a lad, Wentworth always treated Hector as if he were part of a special group, whereas his brothers liked to run off and leave him to play alone. Wentworth had also protected him and Will from their father many times while Stephen was at school. He'd only been a child then, but he was so handsome, strong, and brave that Hector swore nothing would ever keep them from being friends.

Of course, part of that had been a child's fancy, but over the years the craving for his hero's attention turned into the craving for a lover's touch. A child's affection turned into the longings of a man.

Actually, he was barely more than a boy when they came

together for the first time, not long after his twentieth birthday. He'd been lean and insubstantial under Wentworth's weight. But their first month together had been bliss. Wentworth had been more important than life, and he thought Wentworth felt the same. He thought they would be together forever. Forever turned out to be less than one season. After Hector sided with his family, Wentworth left until his position and family business required his return to England.

Hector was surprised and ecstatic to meet him again. With a little trickery, he convinced Wentworth they needed this holiday. He needed a second chance with this extraordinary man, so he made it happen. But the past two days had been strained.

In fact, the past week had not been perfect. Things were uncomfortable between them at times. Except when they made love. That was always good, and it *was* lovemaking. He didn't care if Wentworth couldn't see their coming together was not simply sex. He *knew*, and he cherished their time together.

The smooth glide inside his burning arse brought Hector back to the moment, and it was exactly what he craved.

Wentworth strained. Eyes closed, he pushed his hips up, shoving his prick onto that spot that made Hector squirm.

Hector needed to slow this down, prolong the dreamlike experience. He concentrated on the discomfort of grass and pebbles under his knees to postpone his release, never wanting this moment to end. He leaned forward to taste Wentworth, his mouth touching those strong, parted lips.

Wentworth's eyes flew open, and he pushed Hector back. "No, it is better this way." He released the vise-like grip on his hip, grabbed Hector's rod, and stroked.

Though disappointed to be cheated out of the intimacy, Hector had to agree it felt better. Wentworth's penis hit that spot, the spot he needed to be slammed over and over again.

The spot that made everything else in the world cease to exist, and everything important in the world was right there, in his arse and at the tip of his cock.

He closed his eyes as ecstasy began at the base of his balls and sang through every muscle and fiber of his being. He sighed his release, as anything louder would have detracted from the orgasmic perfection.

Stars exploded behind his closed eyelids, but he missed too much. He wanted to watch Wentworth come, see that beautiful face lost in passion. Yet it was difficult to pull his attention away from his still-spasming rod, squirting come over his embroidered waistcoat. That silk frippery would be ruined.

With half-closed eyes, Wentworth barely looked at Hector. He bucked up into him, tossed his head back and forth, bucked, again, again. Then he came.

Hector could feel Wentworth's cock jumping inside him every few seconds. The aftermath of Wentworth's orgasm was almost enough to make his still-hard organ come again. He lay down, squeezing his member between the two of them, his lover's hard cock inside him. With his head on one firm shoulder, he just absorbed his essence.

Wentworth's member slid out, and a drizzle of come dripped down his scrotum. It tickled, but he didn't care. He was too content. This was paradise.

He'd been with a few lovers since his brief affair with Wentworth; well, three to be exact. The first only lasted for one coupling. The other two affairs had died out over a few weeks from lack of interest of both parties. But none of those men compared with his viscount.

He sat up and propped one elbow on Wentworth's chest. Once again, he suspected he wore a senseless grin, but he couldn't stop the smile.

Wentworth sighed heavily.

"You still have what it takes, old man."

Wentworth growled, grabbed his hand, and kissed it. "I'll show you old man, imp."

Wentworth seized Hector's knee and arm, and before Hector knew what was happening, he was under Wentworth, the smell of fresh spring grass surrounding him. The sunlight shimmered between the poplar trees, throwing dancing shadows. Wentworth looked like a god in human form. He bent and bit Hector's earlobe.

Laughing, Hector pushed, then twisted his head fast for a quick kiss.

Their lips touched.

Wentworth froze, his eyes closed, and his lips trembled. He broke off the kiss, sat up, stood, and then tucked himself in. "Well, look here—you ruined my waistcoat, imp." The flippant comment was not smoothly delivered, and his lover's voice cracked on *imp*.

What the hell was wrong here? Sex was acceptable to his lordship, but anything more intimate was not allowed? "So. My kisses are not good enough? If you think I need more practice, I am up for some tutoring."

Wentworth walked to the horses.

Hector stood and dressed, then followed. "Please, tell me. I know something is wrong. Tell me so we can fix this." He waved vaguely at the crushed grass. "Is it that I sided with my family when…well, when things were falling apart?"

Wentworth turned. His face could have been carved in granite, as much emotion as it showed. "Do you know why you had to side with your family?"

And there was the ridiculous part of this whole affair. No one, not Wentworth, not William, not even Mary had considered him adult enough to tell him the whole tale. Not even after he helped them right a substantial wrong. He'd known so little at the time, he hadn't known what to do and still keep Wentworth as a lover. In retrospect, would he modify his actions to keep Wentworth for himself? Of course he bloody would.

"I knew enough." He hoped his voice conveyed confidence and wisdom and did not sound like a young fool who didn't know his own mind.

"Well, then, my knowledgeable friend, let us go find some food." He gave a charming smile that exuded power. "I am starving. Are you hungry? We can picnic on the east lawn." He launched himself into the saddle.

Hector adjusted his twisted shirt before mounting. They started for the estate to arrange a picnic and toward a day that, for a reason he did not want to consider closely, had turned suddenly gloomy.

Hector intended to alter the climate, and he knew exactly how to achieve that goal.

CHAPTER SEVEN

They laughed as they dismounted and walked toward the entrance of his estate. Hector was ever so clever with retelling an event or a joke. Wentworth had never been clever that way, always worried he could not deliver the humor or irony without appearing awkward. So he did not tell jokes or share humorous tales. Granted, his conversations tended to be one-sided. He was comfortable letting others talk and entertain. Always had been. The navy fit him perfectly in this respect. He learned a great deal as sailors and officers yammered on and on as he listened.

His propensity for few words made his crew jump to when he started issuing orders. It worked to his advantage. Until now. Now he did not seem quick enough, flippant enough, fun enough for his much younger lover.

At that particular moment, watching Hector throw his head back and laugh, the sun gleaming off his dark hair, Wentworth felt old. Serious and hidebound. Was he a pervert for prompting debauchery with a young man? Of course, he should have considered this a few years before now, but...

Here, now, what should he do? What should *they* do?

And then he realized he wanted—no, *needed*—cleverness in his life. He, Grandfather, and Will had all been driven. They weren't averse to fun or humor, but Hector was light and jovial without seeming frivolous. The boy could be a great negotiator or barrister if he set his mind to it and followed that path.

"Wentworth," Hector said exuberantly as they entered the manor, "I need to wash the dust off and will be down for our picnic in a jiff."

"A visitor in your study to see you, my lord," a footman said as he bowed.

Wentworth's blood turned icy. He forced his face to relax into a neutral social expression. It might not be who he feared. Perhaps it was simply the local vicar asking for a donation to improve the grounds of the church. Yes, perhaps Vicar Brown was the caller. Wentworth divested himself of his gloves to hand to the footman.

Hector did the same, and as they left the entry, he whispered, "Send them away as fast as possible. There are so many things we can do this afternoon, I'm fraught to decide which will be the most pleasant."

Struggling past his apprehension about the reason for the call, Wentworth forced a smile for his guest. "Go ahead and change for tea. I am certain I will not be detained long."

The boy rushed off as if he had no other worries in the world.

To be that carefree again. Although, thinking back, he had never felt that lighthearted. Always being studious and responsible for family and friends had made him old at a very young age. He exhaled and let contentment flow through his lungs as he watched Hector dash up the stairs.

When the boy disappeared around a corner, Wentworth headed for the study. He stopped just outside the door, took one deep breath, straightened his jacket, then smoothed his hair before going into the dark paneled room.

He knew who waited for him before he saw the stocky frame outlined by the afternoon sun from the large mullioned windows. He could feel William's presence, had been able to since they were young, like an extension of his own senses.

Back again after only two days. And once again to see him, not his brother.

Stiffening his spine and erasing a frown of concentration, he walked to the center of the room. "William, I am surprised to see you again."

Will faced him.

"What do you want this time? Since I did not accept your offer, I thought I would learn you were back in London."

Will strode to the unlit fireplace, where he turned and stood at attention. His muscles were tense, his hands behind his back, and his expression guarded as if he knew not what to expect. He was handsome as hell. "You know me better than that, Ty. I always get what I want. You have enough experience to realize that much."

"Yes. So, what is your latest desire?"

Will gave a snort and a half smile that set the small hairs on the back of Wentworth's neck standing on end. "What do I want..." He walked to the sun-bright window again. He seemed agitated and could not stand still. "There are so many things I want, Ty. So many."

Wentworth left the center of the room that was so far from Will. He left safety and walked into the lion's den. "Tell me, Will. If I had come to see you yesterday, what would we have spent our time doing? I should not ask, but I find myself beyond curious. Would you have had me beaten?"

Will laughed. "Of course not. You understand me well enough to know I fight my own fights."

"Would you have tried to seduce me?"

Will leaned close, watching Wentworth's mouth. He was so near, Wentworth felt the fresh caress of breath. "Would it have worked if I tried?"

Will stepped back just as Hector flung the door open and stopped dead in his tracks, gaping at them.

"William?"

Will turned and took two steps toward his brother.

"Why are you here, Will?"

"Yes, Will. That seems to be the question on everyone's mind," Wentworth said in agreement.

Will cleared his throat before telling what seemed to be a half-truth. "I came to check on your well-being, Hector. Are you well?"

"Quite, as you can see." Hector stepped out of the doorway and pointed at the exit he just vacated. "Now that you have verified my health, you should leave so I can continue with my holiday."

"I don't suppose I could convince you to leave with me."

Hector shook his head, his beautiful mouth drawn into a deep frown.

Will buttoned his coat and left the room. Hector closed the door as soon as Will cleared the opening. Still facing the door, he asked, "Why was he here?"

There was no reason to lie, so he said, "He is trying to get me to leave you."

Hector sighed. "That meddling bastard."

"Your brother cares about you, and in his way, he is trying to help."

Hector turned to him, his face devoid of emotion. "From where I stood, it appeared he was trying to get you into his bed."

What was there to say after that? *Yes, your brother and I used to be lovers. He broke my heart. I still love him.* No, nothing seemed appropriate, so he said nothing, damning himself and Will with his silence.

When emotion did appear on Hector's face, it was rage. "You cur. You had me in your bed last night, today, and just now you let my brother try to seduce you. How perverted is that?"

"That statement is a great exaggeration, Hector. He wants you to leave and go back to London. And if you had even a smattering of sense, you would see I am a bad influence on you, and you would go back to town with your brother."

"Do you want me to leave?" Hector came to him then, and put his hand on Wentworth's chest, just over his heart.

He did not even have to think about his answer. "No. No, I really do not."

❖

After a morning of hard riding and fucking outdoors, Wentworth should have been starved, but he could only finish half of his salmon with leeks and potatoes. He knew the food was good, considering how much he paid that sullen chef to stay. He'd threatened many times to run off to a neighboring lord's kitchen while in one of his moods. Unfortunately, tonight Wentworth tasted not a single forkful.

He was ashamed of how he'd treated Hector earlier that day in the clearing, and William's visit had disturbed him. He should want to avoid Hector, spend time alone untangling his thoughts. But instead, all his attention fixed on his handsome guest sitting across the informal dining table. Hair neatly arranged, black-and-white attire, impeccable manners, Hector could have been a visiting dignitary or a prince from an exotic land.

The desire, which had tented his trousers for the past hour, started to cause pain. Even though he'd come inside the man earlier that day, he was still poker-hard and wanting more.

The fucking had been good. No, he would not kid himself. The bed play had been fantastic. He wanted more. Now.

Using the table to shield his actions, he reached out a foot and drew Hector's leg toward his. They rubbed calves. He hugged the firm limb between his own.

Hector finished the last two bites of salmon and whispered, "Shall we go upstairs?"

Wentworth stood. "Retire to the study for a glass of port?" he said loudly for the servants' ears, then walked into the fire-warmed study, Hector following.

"Secure the door, Hector."

At the snick of the lock, Wentworth turned slowly. Hector stalked him like a cat with his graceful stride. He was such a gorgeous man. As gorgeous as his brother at the same age—near black curls, full, firm lips, large dark eyes, muscular yet agile.

He and Hector could have made something lasting of their friendship, but Hector already had enough information to realize there was a past love affair with William. It was only a matter of time before all the pieces came together, and then he would leave, not quietly as William had done, but in a ferocious outburst. No, this vibrant soul would sear Wentworth at his exit.

"Port or brandy?"

"Neither. All I want is you."

A shiver Wentworth tried hard to fight quaked his body. So heady, this attention.

Hector moved close and leaned in, tipping his dark, evening-stubbled chin for a kiss. He showed tenacity, that was for certain.

Turning in pretense of removing his cravat, he was not fast enough to avoid seeing the flicker of hurt in Hector's eyes. Of course there would be disappointment. He was being a cad, but there was no way around this issue. Kissing was out of the question. He'd tried.

When they were first together, he liked the fact that Hector looked like William. Loved the fact that Hector smelled like William. Adored the fact that Hector tasted like William.

At first, he thought he found a good substitute for the man he could not have, but then he came to care for the boy deeply. At that point, it had been too late to confess everything. Now it was still too late. And kissing him seemed too intimate, a betrayal of sorts.

After all the damage he'd inflicted on the Somervilles, after his duplicity, the shunning, the christening, William's recent offer—and what the hell had that been an offer of?—it was eons beyond too late. Why had he not confessed when they had first come together? If he had not been a deceitful bastard then, he could kiss Hector now without being reminded of his deceit, and could avoid the fear that once the boy found out…What? What would happen? Would Hector hate him? Yes, most certainly. Would he leave in a fit of temper? Most assuredly. Would he break the boy's heart?

At this very moment, Wentworth hated his obsidian temperament. How could he harm the two boys he'd made a crusade out of protecting?

Each and every kiss hammered home the knowledge that he was a deceiver. He had ignored that at the beginning of this fortnight, but after Will's visit, it was too painful. It hurt. It hurt like bloody hell. Every time he caught a whiff of Hector, his emotions boiled up and his stomach clenched.

Now there was an aphrodisiac for you. He nearly laughed

at his sorry state—what a disaster he was. Of course, he'd been a disaster ever since falling in love with his best friend at fourteen. Pathetic.

Having Hector, a constant reminder of the man he betrayed, the man who would not speak to him for years, the man he never told Hector he had loved, lit a brimstone fire in his soul. Goddamn, he could not resist the young man's body, or his enthusiasm, but must do so without tasting or smelling. For some reason those senses were linked to his memories so tightly, they could transport him back to his darkest times.

He poured himself a shot of brandy and downed it, needing the liquid courage. These damnable melancholy thoughts were destructive. He knew Hector was tired of being treated like a whore and would press for more intimacy.

Hector slipped behind him and helped remove his coat and waistcoat.

Turning, he returned the favor, pulling a bit too hard at the crisp white shirt, wanting him naked now. What a lovely body—young, supple—and he wanted to enjoy it. All of it.

He stayed in shirtsleeves and trousers as Hector stepped out of the rest of his clothing. A proud, blushing cock, curved and long, jutted out of a black nest of pubic hair. Wentworth laid him down on the carpet, intending to suck that proud cock. He'd not given him oral pleasure since their reintroduction, though they had not lacked in inventiveness. He ran his tongue from navel to the crease of one firm thigh and caught a whiff of the night he and Will lost their virginity together.

He sat up and swallowed hard.

Hector opened his eyes and writhed. "God, don't stop. Suck me. I need you to suck me, or I might die of wanting you."

Wentworth looked at the wall, unable to hold his gaze.

Not when he thought of…when he smelled the unmistakable scent of William, knowing he would have to confess but being too cowardly to do it today.

He ran a hand across his face. "No. I have something better planned." What, he did not quite know at the moment, so he gave himself time to think by removing the rest of his clothing. Slowly, an idea came to mind. Not one of his preferred acts, but he had to do something worthwhile for Hector, something better than a suck-off.

"I want you to fuck me."

"Really?" Hector jerked into a sitting position. "We've never…I mean, yes, of course. It would be a great pleasure… if you're certain."

"Very certain. Just be careful, it has been years."

Hector scurried to his trousers for the ointment. "Yes, I will go as slowly as you want. Thank you."

"Hopefully, it will be my pleasure," he said as he lay on his side and raised one leg. He always felt degraded taking it on hands and knees like a mare, and since kissing was out of the question, this position would have to do.

Fingering the plush, intricately decorated wool of the dark-red-and-gold Axminster carpet, he jumped when Hector touched his flank. *Damnation! Get hold of yourself.* He knew this would be good. that it would go as slowly as he needed, but one of the last times he was buggered, his last time with Hector's brother, came to mind. It had been little more than rape with consent. It had been rough, to say the least, not what he'd wanted or expected, and his arse had burned for days after.

"Relax, my love."

Love. Love? With that last word, Wentworth remembered their shared companionship and plans two years ago. Hector had proclaimed his undying love, and he had done…What had he done? He did not remember, but he was certain he had not loved him back. Could he have? Yes, maybe he had.

He let the confusing thought slip from his mind when Hector said, "I won't hurt you. Promise." Hector kept his promise, starting with a kneading caress along his back, legs, and buttocks.

Wentworth took a deep breath and prepared for penetration.

Once fingers started to slick his passage, his suspicion that Hector had experienced sex outside his bed was confirmed. Even though he enjoyed the educated probing, he was not at all certain he liked the fact that Hector had buggered some other man.

After two fingers massaged and opened him, he gently slipped a third in, and all three digits curved to touch his sweet spot. Wentworth moaned.

"Do you like that?"

He nodded.

"Want more?"

He nodded again.

"Tell me."

At this, Wentworth balked. It was fine for his lovers to beg, but he was a viscount, for God's sake—he had never learned how. He shook his head.

Hector's warm tongue ran from the base of his spine to his shoulder blade. He shivered.

"I shall fuck you, Wentworth. And you will scream for me."

Again, he shook his head. This time with more emphasis, and then Hector slipped in. A slick rod wrapped in silk. Hard as ice but smooth and hot. Forbidden. Sinful. Necessary.

Wentworth moaned low as Hector penetrated his arse with his smooth shaft. The burn was so much less than the pleasure squeezing up from his balls that the pain simply added to the delight.

"That's it, love. Moan for me, and soon I will have you screaming."

"Cocky bastard."

Hector laughed, the sound barely audible while sucking on his shoulder with soft lips. Hector then started a slow slide in and out, angled in a way that each stroke rubbed that special spot.

The skin around his hole burned, but he could not stop the cry of desire and want. That spurred Hector to a faster pace. They rocked together, finding a perfect rhythm.

Hector grabbed Wentworth's cock. The release seemed to rip from his arse to his cock, then through his entire body. He yelled, "Yes. Yes. God, yesss."

The pumping in his arse intensified, sped to a frenzied pace, prolonging his orgasm. A million sunsets flashed behind his closed eyes, and for a moment he floated. He feared he would never catch a breath, but then Hector shoved in one last time and hissed a strangled oath. Wentworth came again. That had never happened before.

He lay on the carpet, studying the colorful design around and around its intricate pattern. He felt a bit stupefied. He could not remember the last time he felt this completely and totally fulfilled. He was too relaxed to move.

"Thank you. Thank you for that. God, Wentworth... That was the most...mmm." His member slipped out slowly, causing a deliciously pleasant burn, and Wentworth's arse contracted again, sending an orgasmic aftershock through his body.

"Damnation, Hector, seems you took something integral to my survival just then," he slurred, having trouble forming words.

Hector kissed his flank. "Never fear, you may have it back anytime you wish. Here, let me clean us up."

He smiled and stretched, then allowed Hector to wipe him clean with a handkerchief.

The bliss lasted only a few moments until the familiar disgust seeped in. How could he share this act when he held such a damning secret?

Carefully, he levered himself on one elbow, allowing his body to adjust after being plowed.

Hector knelt and handed over his clothing. "Shall we continue upstairs and make a full night of this?" He admired Wentworth's naked body with a slow, warm slide of his palm on his arse and thigh.

Even disgusted with himself, he could not resist the temptation. He grabbed his shirt and said, "Yes, come to my rooms after eleven. I will dismiss my valet early. We will have the whole night to do as we please."

When he looked up, Hector was too close to avoid. He'd made a tactical advance and forced their mouths together.

The feel of firm masculine lips was delightful and fulfilled a long-held emptiness, until his starved lungs forced him to breathe, and he caught the scent of his first love. It was like kissing a man long dead. He exhaled quickly and tried to continue without breathing, but eventually he had to. He turned his head, but Hector forced their lips together once more. Guilt swamped his senses, and he pushed up from the floor and grabbed the back of a chair. He swallowed, took a deep breath, then swallowed again and again.

Hector's voice slipped up his back like a tentacle from cold Windermere Lake. "Are my kisses so disgusting that they make you ill? You used to kiss me." He said the last quietly, with no heat.

Not at all sure what to say, Wentworth shoved his arms into his shirt.

"I'm good enough to fuck, and finally you allowed me to fuck you, but my kisses make you gag as if you'd just tasted carrion?"

Ignoring the question, he struggled into his trousers, small clothes be damned. "That is ridiculous. You misunderstand."

Hector had obviously reached his limit. "Goddamn you, why won't you kiss me?"

There was no avoiding this. He'd done so for two years, and it was past time, but God, he did not want to face this. He would rather be in front of an angry mob of marines. If he could only think of a way to once again postpone the inevitable. Nothing came to mind, so he turned and shrugged. "I cannot. I just...cannot."

"And why is that?"

Tucking in his shirttails, he admired Hector, still gloriously naked and proud, one leg bent under him, the other crocked up, an arm wrapped around his knee. "Why not, Wentworth?"

He continued dressing.

"Talk to me." The request was soft and quiet, enticing him to stop fighting, to share the truth. He knew this was a very, very bad idea, but Hector deserved to know.

"It is just...just that...you taste like him. You smell like him. God, I cannot separate the two of you with my eyes closed or even half closed, and I did not tell you. I could never figure out how to tell you." He rubbed his gut. Suddenly a hollow, sucking feeling swamped his insides.

"William."

"Yes," he said under his breath, confirming the damning statement, but he was certain Hector already knew the truth.

"You still love him."

He nodded. Of course he still loved Will. They'd been more than lovers; they'd been best friends for years. He would always love Will, but that did not mean—

"And when he wouldn't have you any longer, you took second best. You took me."

Was that what he had done? He said nothing while he wrestled with his thoughts and tried to remember memories long buried.

"Damn. Damn, damn, damn." On his feet faster than Wentworth could blink, Hector said, "I've lived in my brothers' shadows my entire life. I was ever such a smug bastard thinking I'd achieved something Will never could. And now you do this to me?" The look on his face was murderous.

He prepared for the blow as Hector stalked up to him. He closed his eyes and waited. He knew he deserved a good thrashing, but no punches were delivered.

Opening one eye just a slit, he saw Hector's face distorted with rage.

"What about before?"

Wentworth knew what that cryptic question meant. As much as he hated to hurt Hector further, it was time to stop hiding the truth from him as well as from himself.

"Before, I planned to tell you, but I could not determine how to do so. I loved him for years, while you were just a child. He was my world. Then I lost him. He left me." *I lost the one thing that meant most in the world to me, and it crushed me.* "I cared for no one else until...I fear that you will...Bloody hell." He jabbed fingers through his hair and shook his head.

"I. Love. You." Hector's face contorted into fury, belying the words, but Wentworth knew he spoke true. "I love you, and he never will. He cannot."

He had once. Now Wentworth pushed that thought away

because it no longer mattered. With an ache in his heart, he remembered something long buried. He remembered the first time he lost a lover and his life changed forever.

❖

Winter 1797, Kent

"Ty?" His name was so softly spoken.

Tyler jumped at the light touch on his shoulder, though he had expected it. Even so, the contact made his heart race.

They might have time to sneak up to the small bedroom for a hearty goodbye before Will returned to school and he went back to the navy. No one would know.

He would know, and he already had trouble sleeping at night, reliving the wonderful things they did in warm, sweaty darkness. He wanted one more memory to add to his collection before he shipped out again.

He pulled his coat tight against the icy northern breeze and turned toward Will. The idiot was out in this weather without an overcoat. "You must be freezing out here. How long have you been standing there? It is so blasted dark, it is a wonder neither of us fell in the pond. Cannot see a bloody thing."

He leaned into Will, warm breath tickled his ear, and he took advantage of the light clothing to caress Will's arms slowly. Shivers coursed through his frame.

Forcing himself to act rationally, he ignored his urge to take him right there in the frosted park. "Come upstairs to your room with me, and I shall warm you. We have time before the moon rises and I have to leave."

He slid fingers into Will's hair. Will tilted his head and quietly moaned. A hot surge of lust renewed his temptations.

He shook off the lurid thoughts and pulled Will toward the manor.

"I cannot. Not again."

"Oh, playing coy, Will? We had grand fun last night. Did we not?" Grand fun was an understatement. Last night had been heaven, except for some reason, Will kept his eyes tightly closed for the first time, even as his body responded with enthusiasm.

"Last night I was in my cups and lost my better judgment. I made a decision but was too weak to tell you. It cannot happen again." Will cleared his throat and pulled his arms away, leaving a cold, empty void where Will's warm body had recently been fitted against his.

Will leaned against the short granite garden wall and looked toward the distant lights of crofters in the valley below the estate grounds.

Tyler did not, would not, give up something this important to his existence. He closed in and stepped into Will's warmth, his chest and thighs pressing gently against back and legs. He wrapped his arms around Will's firm waist and leaned his head on his broad shoulder. "Do not be silly. You were in your cups last night, but not all the nights prior. We have played for years. You know I can make you feel good." He demonstrated with hands that knew Will's body as well as he knew his own, sliding a gentle touch up and under Will's dinner jacket.

Will shivered but turned and grabbed Ty's wrists firmly, turning their intimate contact aggressive.

"This will hurt us both, but it has to be done. I do care for you, Ty. I love you in some kind of fashion, just not enough. And damn it, this must stop. At some point we will get caught, and then there will be hell to pay. What we had was fun. We were friends who were too young to know better, then old enough to know better but too young to attract women. I've grown out of

that youthful phase where I need to experiment, and we both need to go and find more out of life."

Tyler started to tremble. His knees barely supported him. "You are all I want out of life, Will."

"Damn it, Ty. I'm only eighteen. I want a normal existence, pursuing research as a physician into the causes and cures of disease, an appointment to the Royal Society as a scientist, a marriage my family will be proud of, and children."

"We could be together and—"

"No, we cannot be together, and you know it. Stop deluding yourself."

"I love—"

"But I don't love you the same way. And we cannot marry." *He laughed. "Imagine what Stephen...Hell, forget about my brother. What would society say if I brought you home as my wife?"*

"Now you are just being ridiculous." Tyler gasped, struggled for breath. Neither of them had to play the woman.

"I feel like the biggest type of cretin, but this must be done."

Tyler stared where he knew ebony eyes were hidden by the dark. "Don't do this, Will."

"Go toy with someone else. I do not want you. I lust after women, Ty. More than I ever thought possible as we were growing up."

A sob ripped from Tyler's throat. He knew there was no changing Will's mind. He'd been pulling away for months.

He reached with one hand and touched Will's beloved face, the skin moist with tears. He leaned forward and gave him a gentle goodbye kiss more symbolic of their ended relationship than of a physical separation. For God's sake, the two of them had seen each other almost daily for the past nine years, except when he was training at sea and Will had classes. They would likely be forced together often for the next ten as well, when Will graduated and was stationed with him.

This was goodbye to his one chance at love. Will, with a crazy lack of judgment, had decided for both of them, and it hurt like a cannon blast to his chest.

"I have to be strong and stop this insanity before we ruin everything. After all, it is simply boyhood lust. A fun fuck here or there. Nothing more. It cannot be more. It's wrong, Ty. Unnatural. Men who continue to do this after they grow up are abominations. The longer they participate in sodomy, the more unstable they turn. Eventually they are not fit to be around children."

"Did you read this in one of your medical texts?" he asked, mocking his friend.

"In fact, yes. And I don't want anyone to find out about us. Promise to never tell anyone, Ty." Will shoved both hands in his pockets. To keep from reaching out again, or to keep from physically shoving Tyler away with more than just words? "See you soon, eh?"

Tyler's fist flashed out before he knew what he intended. The blow zipped through the dark with such stinging accuracy, Will stumbled backward, tripped over something, and landed on the frosted grass.

He was halfway to the stables before registering the startled, "Ty?"

The dampness on his cheeks surely came from the night's dew.

❖

"I always wondered why you sabotaged William's happiness," Hector said. "Now it makes sense. You wanted him all to yourself. Well, turns out you received nothing. How does that feel?"

It feels like crawling through a mile of fresh goat shit, actually.

"You loved my brother first. You fucked my brother first, and you did not think that was important to tell me?" Hector turned away, then turned back, his face red with anger. "I repeat, I love you, and he cannot. He never will. Get the hell over him before you ruin what we might have together. I have adored you since I was a child. Am I only a substitute body for you? Am I?" Tears welled in Hector's lovely dark eyes, his whole body shaking, fists clenched.

Wentworth looked at him. Truly looked. He was gorgeous in his fury, dark curls in disarray, but his eyes were full of love, and that scared the devil out of him.

He could love Hector. Had probably loved him at one time. Hell, he could not remember. Damnation, he was getting a headache trying to sort this out…this…whatever the hell it was.

He wanted to be happy with a man. With this man. But it was not right. How he felt was too strong, his emotions too entwined with this family, and he could not live through another rejection if he let his heart have free rein.

He would allow himself stolen moments, lust, longing, affection for a lifetime, but not love. Love was too painful. They could have a brief affair. Be occasional lovers. Nothing more.

No happily ever after.

No forever.

It was not possible for people like them.

Will had taught him that when he left that cold Grantham winter night. The message was driven home again when Will's vitriol and hatred at learning Wentworth slept with Hector turned into a violent assault.

Understandable, really, since Wentworth had tainted a young man of twenty and had never been brave enough to tell either brother. That deception still burned a hole in his heart. He swallowed a lump at the reminder.

Will would not have had such a horrified reaction if the act of sodomy were not so heinous in the eyes of society. Because of constant pressure and cajoling, Will had tried sodomy. Although they both enjoyed it for some time, in the end it had nearly ruined their friendship. Sleeping with Hector, betraying the family, *did* ruin their friendship. Will and his wife were filling a nursery, just what a man should do. The natural progression in life.

God, his thoughts were all jumbled. He turned away from Hector, trying to clear his mind. He felt stupid and confused. He needed time to think, but Hector kept pushing.

"Talk to me!"

He spat careless words, hoping to gain time. "This is not love. We are sating lust, that is all. We can have fun for a while, but nothing more." Realizing what he said was an unmitigated lie, he ran fingers through his hair and forced a calm he did not feel. "I do enjoy your company. Stay the fortnight. We shall ride again tomorrow if you like."

"So, by the end of next week you will break my heart? Is that what I must look forward to?" Hector's voice shook as if his heart did not need to wait an extra week before shattering.

Wentworth almost reached out for him then. He did not want anyone to ever feel the pain that had nearly ruined him a decade ago, but he could not touch the lad. Out of self-preservation, he kept his distance.

"I want you," Hector said. "Not just for a fortnight, but

forever. Don't you see this is something special? We could make a life for ourselves. You and I could be together, be a kind of family. I know men who have succeeded in this." He reached out a trembling hand.

He wanted to accept that hand and the offer with all that was inside him, but Hector was fanciful. He needed a dose of reality, so Wentworth lashed out instead. "Don't be ridiculous. Two men living together do not make a family!" He laughed. It was not a happy sound. "Do not delude yourself."

"We can make it work. We must simply be discreet."

"You do not understand." He shook his head. "So naïve…"

"Naïve? I am too good for you, sir. I refuse to be second best." Saliva sprayed on the last, heated word. "I will find a man who wants a life with me because he loves me. And you can rot in the pathetic world you created for yourself."

Hector gathered his clothes, jamming arms and legs into shirt and pants with no regard to seams or tender skin.

"Be sensible and do not leave in a fit. The servants will talk."

Cravat poking out of one pocket, hair sticking up on one side, Hector turned and gave him a rather vulgar hand gesture. Probably the most vulgar thing the boy had ever learned. He then turned on his heels and stormed out of the room, angry footsteps echoing off the teak floor.

Wentworth wanted nothing more than to bellow his words to the entire household, but he contented himself with raw mutters. "I should have kept my damn mouth shut. I knew he would not take the truth well."

He'd protected his heart since the reunion with Hector, so why did he feel the boy's absence so sharply? Because he wanted, no, *needed* Hector. He ached for the boy to return. He would talk to him in the morning and apologize. Perhaps by then his mind would be clear of all these half-formed thoughts, and he could start making sense out of his jumbled feelings.

Yes, tomorrow Hector would be calm, and they would work out this problem.

CHAPTER EIGHT

Hector brought the bay mare to a walk. No reason to take his foul mood out on the sturdy horse. It wasn't her fault Wentworth was a bastard.

Wiping sweat from his forehead, he squinted at the orange sun blazing halfway up over the horizon. It would be a hot day. It was already warm even in the shade of the large oaks lining the dirt road. The horse would need water soon.

He trembled with anger, thinking about last night's confrontation.

He'd left at daybreak, would have left the night before had it been a full moon. He'd demanded a horse with good stamina be saddled, and he'd taken only his leather money purse and stormed from the cursed Kent estate. Fearing Wentworth would catch up to him, placate him, and seduce him into staying the rest of the fortnight, he'd not even taken the time to exchange horses at his family estate. And there was the off chance he might see William, and in his current mood, he might try to kill his brother. So he left as fast as possible, and it felt like he was fleeing.

In fact, his exodus had been so rushed, he'd forgotten to ask the horse's name. Poor girl.

Wentworth was a bastard! Damn, it kept coming back to

that. Hector's judgment in regard to the men he fancied was dreadful. Why couldn't he have fallen for someone stable, like Lord Blair had when he found his Captain Wedgewood?

And Hector had known better, since Wentworth already broke his heart once before. Still, he'd coordinated this sojourn into hell with eyes open and his heart on a salver, even knowing why Wentworth left the country. He'd been too ashamed of plotting malfeasance against the Somerville family to remain on good, clean English soil. After spilling the truth about cooperating with a demented man obsessed with Mary just to keep her from marrying Will, Wentworth signed his ship up for patrol after patrol. He overtaxed himself, his vessel, and his crew, and for what purpose? Punishment for his actions? Fear of retaliation?

Hector sided with the family; he'd had to. Wentworth's actions almost led to Mary's death, not that he'd known Admiral Greig was demented, but still he'd lied to Will, to Hector, to all of them. The man had done something unconscionable, so of course Hector sided with his family.

To be sure, he was an idiot to give the man a second chance, and Wentworth was a bastard. A fucking bastard.

He remembered the last time he'd seen Wentworth before he left the country, the day he learned how agonizing a broken heart could be.

For years he'd had a niggling suspicion wrapped around his chest that William and Wentworth were once lovers, but he stupidly believed that if they did have a liaison, it had been out of convenience and so lacked in importance. But when he saw the two men fight and wrestle on the floor on that winter day, they'd looked so much like they were mimicking the act of love. They were the closest of friends, who had helped each other through an abusive father, through war, and through love and lost love. But were they still lovers?

He'd always been jealous of Wentworth's affection for Will, but he never truly believed Will had returned that affection. He'd never believed they were in love.

On that day almost two years ago, the small, wiggling green emotion in his chest ignited, and Hector turned into something he was ashamed of. When he observed the two men struggling on the floor, his bones felt fluid, his muscles on fire, and he could easily have killed them both on the spot—right there on the floor, struck them down when Wentworth's lips brushed against Will's ear.

He remembered wondering if they were lovers, something Wentworth confirmed yesterday. Were they still occasional lovers? Damn it coming back to that. No. No. He did not believe that for a moment. Will was too infatuated with Mary to stray.

That horrible night in Grantham, watching his brother and lover fight through a red haze, he'd shoved Mary away. Laughing as he realized he'd been trying to keep her away from the fighting men. He'd scoured the room for a weapon to do both men harm. For a few horrible seconds, he'd been angry enough to kill.

While he searched, Will and Wentworth had lost strength and stopped throwing punches, but they continued their verbal sparring. Their bodies writhed together as if the motions were choreographed, long practiced.

Fortunately, Mary had stopped Hector before he could lay his hands on the large earthenware urn by the door. Otherwise, he would have likely smashed it over both men's heads and spent the rest of his life in gaol.

Hector rubbed more sweat from his face with a violent flick of his thumb.

What a bastard!

Wentworth. Will too, for that matter.

Unmitigated fucking bastards! May they both rot in hell!

He swallowed bitter anger to keep from spurring the horse to a gallop, and patted her neck. The poor girl seemed to be aware of his tumultuous emotions and pranced worriedly, ears twitching and tail flicking. "It's okay, girl. You're a wonderful horse, and I promise to get you extra grain when we arrive in London."

Hector planned to stable the horse at his brother's London residence. He'd flung a note on the bed in his room asking for his things to be sent there, where they could also retrieve the horse.

There was a stream not half a mile ahead. With shaking hands, Hector brought the mare to a trot. Once they both slaked their thirst, he mounted. They should arrive home within the next two hours. By then he hoped to have his emotions—no, his anger at Wentworth, at Will, and at himself reined in.

CHAPTER NINE

Early summer 1808, London

Hector leaned his head against the padded carriage interior, feeling as if his bones had turned to porridge as he watched the upper-class neighborhood change into a very small middle-class one, which then turned into lower-class housing.

Not quite comfortable, he propped his chin in his hand because he didn't have the will to hold his head up as the conveyance rocked over the cobblestones, en route to inspect another business. The fourteenth that week.

Third sons without land had few, if any, legitimate opportunities. And being the *way* he was, he didn't have the option of marrying an heiress. Well, he supposed he could, but he wouldn't subject some poor woman to a chaste match.

He'd been saving as much of his allowance as he could over the past four years, not spending it like most of the young bucks at gaming halls and on loose women. That last part made him laugh. The sound disappeared into the padded carriage interior as if the mirth never existed.

Good thing he had the will to laugh at himself these days, for he certainly had not laughed at anything else the past month. Not since he'd stormed out on Wentworth. Not since leaving his own soul trampled, his heart buried in Kent.

Upon returning to London, he tallied all his savings and investments and asked his friends, Lord Blair and Captain Wedgewood, who'd made bundles on their joint shipping venture, for a small loan. Then he started looking at businesses to purchase. Which venture was not important as long as it let him use his talent for numbers. Keeping accounts, analyzing costs, and studying population growth had always fascinated and come easy for him. He would organize the venture as a company within a company, as his name could never be associated with trade. It wasn't fashionable for a member of the Ton to be involved in trade, but who gave a damn? It was unlikely anyone would find out, anyway.

He'd had this idea several years ago and talked to a less-than-scrupulous lawyer on how to structure the transaction. He decided it would be a lark at worst, profitable at best. And it would fill his mind with thoughts other than one dark-haired viscount.

He had hopes for the factory he headed to look at now, and he'd fabricated an event as an excuse to use the family carriage for this trip. It should make a very good impression on the owner. The family-owned manufacturing company made simple porcelain and ceramic kitchenware; nothing fancy, but highly functional and much needed for a growing lower- and middle-class populace.

Profits would be slow but steady if managed properly. Of all the enterprises Hector had screened, this was the one he held the most hope for. It should at least be able to fund his simple needs in life so he would not have to beg his eldest brother for additional monies if he needed anything. Besides, times were changing, and some peers had switched to investing out of necessity. His decision was not completely unique, but he had not confided in his brothers. In fact, he had avoided William since the confrontation at Wentworth Manor.

Initially, he planned to take this step in a few years when he had sufficient funds to purchase the business outright, but he needed an occupation so he would stop moping about.

Wentworth had written him eight letters. The letter Hector wrote, in which he insisted that Wentworth stop communicating with him, was posted this morning. Pouring all his anger on paper, he let Wentworth know in vitriolic prose that he would never talk to him again. Perhaps what he wrote had been cruel, but he couldn't find it in himself to feel bad about sharing his feelings. If Wentworth's letters had contained any warmth... but they were so technical, so cold. There was no affection bleeding off the page even though that word decorated the page like a dark-inked lie.

The carriage turned a sharp corner into a lower-class section of town. He paid more attention. This is where his employees would come from if he purchased the porcelain works. He was relieved to see the residents obviously cared about their neighborhood—the streets were somewhat clean, most of the rubbish and horse dung swept, flower pots on windowsills, houses well maintained. The people who lived here would have pride in their work, their livelihood.

Hector's mood began to lift. For the first time in thirty-six long days, he felt enthusiastic about the future.

They stopped in front of a nondescript one-story building constructed of utilitarian materials, nothing fancy, which was what one wanted in a business. Put all the money in the product, not the building itself. Hector smiled.

An hour later, after looking at the workings of the business and checking the books of account, he decided to have his solicitor compare the books with the receipts to ascertain everything was as it seemed.

He backed out of the humid, hot building onto the sun-warmed street and dried his forehead with his sleeve, sharing goodbyes with the owner, Mr. Tennyson, a gray-haired man with stooped shoulders and a broad smile. Two more steps back, and he came up against what felt like a brick wall, but the brick wall grabbed his arms. Shaking off the unwelcome grasp, he turned and crouched, preparing to protect his valuables and his life.

Standing feet apart, head tipped down in apology, lips turned up in unmistakable invitation, loomed a Northumberland warrior. Red-blond hair—too long—whipping in the wind, blue eyes pale as if bleached from the sun, and a ruddy face, testament to years spent…patrolling the uplands perhaps.

Hector was, as usual, overly romantic. Had been told that over and again while growing up, but right now, he didn't care. The comparison seemed to fit. Until he opened his mouth to speak.

"Terribly sorry, chap, terribly sorry. Not looking where I was going. You're all right, then?" The sounds of educated London on his voice ruined the upland fantasy.

But that was not so terrible. He was still stunning. Not Wentworth gorgeous, of course, nobody else in the world was that gorgeous, but handsome in a different way. A way that didn't even compare. Tall, fit, with a feral white-toothed smile.

Stepping forward and keeping options for the future completely open, he introduced himself.

Perhaps one day this would be a man he could like. But then, he would have to settle for like, wouldn't he? Because he would never be in love again.

CHAPTER TEN

"Well, that should do the deed quite nicely. No one needs know you are a man of business unless you deem to tell them," Uncle Vincent said as he sanded the thick vellum, his coal-black hair gleaming in the light of the candelabra.

Aunt Elizabeth, Liz to her family, laughed merrily. "Oh, Hector, dear. You shall thrive as a man of business with your own source of income and a profession to stretch your mind. I will admit, at one time, I had hoped you or one of your brothers might share my interest in inventing and apprentice with me, but since none of you had the good sense to become a scientist, I believe this is the best course of action you can take."

Hector smiled at his grandfather's half cousin. She wasn't actually an aunt, but close enough he and his brothers had always called her thus. The woman must be in her sixtieth year, if not more, but she still held a quick mind, and her tall, thin frame vibrated with energy. The only sign of aging was a splash of gray in her vibrant red hair, along with lines around her mouth and eyes from a life spent smiling.

"Uncle, you are so very clever putting this deal together and keeping my name off the contract. It is convenient having a solicitor in the family, especially one who does not allow the rules to get in his way." Hector chuckled. "Thank you. And thank you both for helping me with this endeavor. I'm afraid the rest of the family may well have turned their noses up at me for even suggesting such a thing."

Vincent stood and stretched his brawny frame that appeared unaltered by time. Must be his Gypsy blood. "I do not receive many interesting transactions anymore, so this was a pleasure. Now, it is late, and feels like there will be rain soon. Would you care to stay the night, Hector? Randall and Wedgewood will be here for breakfast, and I believe you haven't seen them in...Well, how long has it been? They were at the christening, I hear. Did you see them there?"

Looking around the opulent office with its crimson brocade overstuffed chairs, expensive carpets, and even more expensive art, Hector absorbed all the remembered familial love and remembered so many happy times he spent here. And for some reason, that brought unhappiness swamping his being. "I had tea with them very recently, but I did not see them at the naming party." Randall and his devoted friend David were easily two of Hector's favorite people, along with Aunt Liz, of course. "They were at the christening, but...I, um, left before they arrived."

"Oh, my poor dear. Why the drooping shoulders? You should be elevated by your coup over London's snobbish aristocrats. Why so sad?"

He did not want to talk about this, but the whole sad story slipped out anyway, as if emotions instead of reason controlled his mouth. He finished his story with, "And there is no expression of love in the letters, only a justification of behavior and apologies for secrecy."

"Hector. I am terribly sorry for your grief."

And that was it. It was grief once more; not anger, not sorrow, but grief, deep and raw and all-consuming.

Aunt Liz squeezed his hand, and Vincent said, "Best way to get over rejection from a wholly unworthy personage is to always keep a more worthy person in the parlor, even if the lost one in the bedroom is still haunting you."

"Vincent St. John, what the devil has gotten into you? It is not like you to spout inconsiderate, typical male drivel."

"One day, Hector, you will find your person for the parlor and the bedchamber. Just as I have." He grasped Aunt Liz's hand and kissed her knuckles. She blushed as brilliantly as a debutante.

Hector found himself blushing as well, wholeheartedly approving of their love, even if half the family refused to acknowledge their union on account of Vincent's mixed blood.

He decided he could leave them with a bit of hope for his sorry state, even if he didn't feel propitious himself. "On a happier topic, I do have an admirer. Afraid I don't know what to do about the attraction yet, but it does help one's opinion of oneself. We've had tea together a number of times and attended a play."

Uncle Vincent gave a wicked grin. "That's the spirit, my man. Grab this lady and take her—"

"Vincent!" Aunt Liz chastised. "Do not finish that thought unless you want to sleep in the garden tonight."

Vincent chuckled. "Right, then. Hector, I am certain you can figure out what to do with your lady admirer."

Aunt Liz saw him to the door, then whispered in his ear as she gave him a hug. "Do not mind your uncle, Hector. We will accept whomever you decide to love." She let him go, and Hector walked down the steps to the street, feeling as if the world shifted under his feet and he had nothing to hold on to.

❖

The threatening rain held off, and Hector had a dry walk home. He even noticed a purpose in his step for the first time since leaving Wentworth Manor. It was always good to see Vincent and Elizabeth, longtime family friends as well as distant relatives. She was a bluestocking and her husband encouraged her, which was a refreshing change from most of the rest of his family.

With a slight smile tugging his lips, he remembered the time Elizabeth allowed him and his brothers to snatch a glimpse of her laboratory. It was a basement room, humid and cold. Little pots steamed on a large wooden table. He'd been very young, and the tour had terrified him. He'd spent a fortnight with troubled dreams. To this day, he remembered every detail of the workroom, could probably even render it with paper and charcoal. He quivered, although now the memory of that space gave him a pleasant shiver, not one of fear. However, he could not understand how Elizabeth spent all day down in that dank room.

"The better to contain fires and explosions if they should occur," she'd once told him. Vincent had added, "*When* they occur, Hector, not *if*." He shivered again and quickened his step.

He turned the corner onto his street. A person lurked by the entry to his rented rooms. Stopping, he looked over his shoulder, wondering if he should retreat, when a familiar voice called him.

"Hector, is that you?"

Lieutenant Baker? What the devil was he doing standing around in the dark?

Baker raised the basket in his hand. "I was about town and realized I'd not had time for supper. I thought perhaps you might be hungry as well. Care for a bite?"

At that moment, Hector's stomach rumbled, and they both laughed.

"Very thoughtful of you. Will you come inside?"

He unlocked the outside door and led Baker upstairs to his rooms. Baker climbed the stairs just one riser behind Hector, so close he could feel his warmth. He shivered for the third time that night.

When they stopped in front of his door, he turned and looked up at Baker. He had paid careful attention to his appearance, it seemed. Freshly shaven, with a crisp cravat and a smile that seemed to promise delights beyond what was in his basket. Hector swallowed. "Forgive the mess. I didn't expect a guest tonight." And with that, he let them both in.

Baker looked around and whistled. "This is a very nice, comfortable home. How many rooms?"

Hector was proud of his slice of London, although he'd changed little since the previous occupants left. He gave his guest the tour. The place was not really in disarray since Hector had a housekeeper, who also made tea and simple meals. Baker's praise warmed him and added to the contentment that started at Vincent's home.

Baker grabbed Hector's hand and brought it to his mouth. "You have made this floor into a welcoming home."

Hector brought his other hand to the lapel of the lieutenant's coat. He was ready for this dinner together, and even more, he realized he was ready for the man in the parlor.

❖

The ocean-blue sky disappeared into the ocean-blue water. There would be a storm soon—any sailor worth his salt could feel the changes in the air around him and know they were in for a rough few days. Wentworth loved a good storm; perhaps the thrill of beating the elements would bring him back to sanity.

Damnation, but the past month had been a challenge. He was angry at himself for treating a vibrant lad so shabbily, his emptiness hurt like a knife wound, and then the damnable memories flooded his every waking moment and most of his dreams as well. How had he ignored, no, *forgotten*, the past so thoroughly that he actually believed the few flickers of remembrances were akin to something his mind made up, not something he had orchestrated, then lived and suffered through?

How he longed to forget again. He did not like, did not respect, the man he had become, and he could not do one blasted thing to correct his bloody fool past decisions. He needed a distraction. Some adventure.

When had the flickers of vague remembrances become a flood of real-life memories? He tried to recall. At Wentworth manor, with Hector, yes, but before that even. When, then? Damn, he did not know. Was it important? Was anything important now that he knew what a pathetic person he was? Now that Hector was gone? Now that Will, once a friend closer than a brother, would never speak to him again?

Ah, there you are. Off to the north northeast, the smallest amount of white lined the hidden clouds beneath. On their present course and with the prevailing wind, they should hit rough water by nightfall and should be in the middle of a squall before middle watch.

He smiled.

❖

"That should just about do it, sir." Mr. Tennyson, the previous owner of the porcelain factory and now Hector's foreman, stacked another plate on a workbench, ready for packing. He had agreed to help Hector for a month as he learned the business, but after seeing the way production and profits improved, he'd stayed seven months so far and did not hint of leaving anytime soon. He claimed he enjoyed seeing his life's work surpass every expectation.

"Very nice indeed, Mr. Tennyson. This batch of plates are our best yet."

"Only because you had the idea to hire an artist. Odd to think that with just a little bit of frippery, our goods fly off the shelves as if by magic." He gave a deep, contented laugh.

Hector had made very few changes to the business, but these alterations nearly doubled their profits. The artist made their affordable crockery appeal to the eye, a new and more durable glaze set the designs, and purchasing clay from a different vendor who supplied a more consistent product gave their tableware an advantage over the others available for sale. They had not even needed to raise the price of their wares because the increased sales covered the slight increase in cost for adding quality.

Running his finger over a newly created plate to feel the smooth, even gloss of the surface, Hector sighed. "I will leave the rest of this run to you, Mr. Tennyson. I'm already late for tea with an associate."

"Righto, sir."

The hiss and pop of the kilns filled the factory, and the employees' conversations were mere buzzing in the background. Hector removed his apron and went to collect his coat.

Hurrying out onto the snow-slick street, he looked for

a hackney, knowing he was not likely to find any until he reached the busier thoroughfares. Damn, but he was late. Jonathan would not be pleased. Hector formulated an excuse as he walked.

For the first time, he wondered why Jonathan had become a chore.

CHAPTER ELEVEN

Early spring 1809, Kent

Wentworth stared at the neatly penned columns trying to make sense of the numbers, but it was hopeless. The past few hours he'd accomplished nothing. Every time he tried to concentrate, memories of large, brown eyes clouded his vision and the numbers on the parchment pages in the leather-bound accounts book blurred.

Disgusted with himself, he shoved the ledger so hard, it slipped from the desk and fell onto the carpet with a dull thud. He pinched the bridge of his nose to relieve the tension building in his head.

Over the last eight months, he had called on the boy every time his *Dragon* docked in Portsmouth, but Hector was never home to him. The many letters he'd sent Hector remained unanswered. When the footman he'd dispatched requested a response, the boy apparently looked at the missive, tossed it on a table in the entryway, said, "I have no reply," and then left for a walk.

Wentworth would show up unannounced again if he thought for one second Hector would spare a word for him, but it was hopeless. They seemed to be truly done with one another.

He had damaged Hector's adoration to the point nothing would ever help. Had he thought something involving champagne, a diversion, and a heartfelt apology would wash away the hurt he'd caused?

The past months had been so unbearably painful that even now he hardly noticed the perfect sunny weather. He missed that imp. The easy smile, the gentleness, the love freely given.

He missed knowing Hector would be there any time, every time he wanted something: to talk, touch, fuck. God, he missed it all. If he were truthful, he would even admit he missed himself, the way he was around Hector. Well, the good side of him around Hector, not the stupid, sullen him who could not bring himself to yield to their affection.

What the hell was wrong with him? When had he turned sentimental?

It was the melancholy that plagued him, that clouded his mind for years, but now memories came rushing back. Half-formed images now took bold shape. The recollections were not flattering. He was a stupid bastard who could not stop thinking about the time he did the rashest thing in his whole sordid life. The time when, he now realized, his heart broke for the second time.

❖

December 18, 1806, Grantham

Seconds after the fight with Will, exhausted, sore, and emotionally raw, Wentworth decided to clear his conscience despite the audience. After all, things could not possibly get any worse.

Hector and Mary prowled around the sitting room, setting

chairs, tea table, chess set back to rights, which the scuffle had disturbed. Will stood over him, hands on his hips.

On his knees, blood dripping from his nose, Wentworth whispered so quietly, he knew no one but Will would hear the confession. "To think I helped Admiral Greig wed Mary off to that drunkard son of his. Got you out of the way so her father would force her to marry Greig. I did it for us, you know, so that I could keep you, but that is not how I lost your love, is it?"

He hoped to never see an expression like the one of pure hatred on Will's face ever again.

Will delivered a powerful, unexpected punch to his jaw that left him dazed.

Hector knelt next to him after Will dragged Mary from the room.

"What did you say? Why did he hit you?"

His laugh gurgled with blood. "I deserved it." And he told Hector part of the truth, leaving out the most important point. The fact that he'd made sure Will was unattached so that Wentworth would not lose his friend and former lover.

A half hour later, after Hector cared for Wentworth's injuries and had given him a tumbler of whisky for the pain, Hector told him they were through.

"I cannot stay with a man who cheated my family," Hector said, his voice vibrating with emotion.

Wentworth held out his hand. "Stay with me. You don't know how rare it is for people like us to find companionship."

"Why did you do it? Why did you conspire against Will's happiness?"

"That was almost three years ago. Back then, I was still young enough to be stupid. Especially since I was grieving for Grandfather. He'd passed only the week prior. Forget the

scene. Stay and forgive me. We have something good together. Stay."

Hector turned his back. "I feel like there is a gaping, bleeding hole in my heart. I want you so badly, but I cannot abide your actions." He swallowed. "You sabotaged his happiness. How could you live with yourself? How could you make love to me knowing what you did? You have put me in a position no one should ever have to tolerate."

There was a glimmer in Hector's beautiful eyes as he turned. He sniffed and rubbed his sleeve against his face, his shoulders hunched.

Wentworth's eyes were moist, and his glass shook. He reached out a beseeching hand, longing for Hector to accept it, to come near and tell him everything would be fine. That he was forgiven.

Instead of clasping the offering, Hector turned, his shoulders back, and with determined steps, he left. Pain that could topple a giant ripped through Wentworth's chest.

❖

Wentworth, so hungry to forget the past, had in fact forgotten. Or more precisely, refused to remember. Remembering their parting doubled the nerve-gnawing guilt that plagued him for years.

Time to put the melancholy and loneliness behind him. It was a ridiculous state in which to wallow. He needed something to take his mind off things. A way to banish the feeling that there was no reason to wake up each day. Not being able to see or touch Hector. His sunshine.

Perhaps that was part of the problem. Maybe the boy was important to his survival, his disposition, his happiness.

What the bloody hell? I am going mad. No. I went mad years ago. There was no reason at all for these maudlin thoughts. For a certainty, the boy had created a nice diversion, but he'd refused Wentworth. It was time to get on with his life. If only he could force himself to think of something other than Hector. Coming back to his estate, where he and Hector had fucked, had been a mistake. For the past handful of days, he had been unable to concentrate on the accounts or anything else, for that matter. That beautiful, sculpted, young body came to mind every time he closed his eyes.

"Hell and castration."

He'd walked around half-erect most of the time Hector occupied his home. Even now, he expected to have the lad appear in the hall, in his study, in his bed. It would not happen. He'd burned that bridge spectacularly.

He prided himself on being a good tactician, so he made himself face the facts. He and the Somerville family were through. Totally and completely through.

Wentworth retrieved and stowed the accounts book he'd been attempting to work on in an oak chest along with his other business papers. He had always been a man who made a decision and stuck by it. This odd indecisiveness would drive him insane. Time to seize the present with both hands and wring a better future for himself out of the ether.

Walking around the room, he purposefully touched each and every artifact from his travels. A brass elephant from India, a walking cane with a hidden ivory-handled sword from Spain, a porcelain plate from Portugal, and the elaborate paper dragon from China. Especially China. His hand lingered on the dragon, which matched the colors of his Axminster carpet.

A bruising ride to Kent, just for the hell of it, would be the first thing. He would clear his mind with activity, then focus on laying precise goals for the next year. A sound idea. That was the way to proceed.

He looked out the window to the sunny meadows as a knock rattled the dark-paneled door. Annoyed at the interruption, he said much too loudly, "Enter."

Smith entered, immaculately turned out as usual, his posture ramrod straight. The only thing out of place on his butler was the enormous beak of a nose.

With ringing, imperious tones, he announced, "Lieutenant Baker of the *Fearless* to see you, my lord."

Oh, now, what's this? He had not seen Red Jon, as the midshipmen called him, in more than a year. This could be the diversion he needed. "Send him in, Smith."

He rubbed his hands together and walked to his desk, straightened his waistcoat, and posed with one hand on a leather backed chair just as the large lieutenant stalked in.

Wentworth believed the sunset-blond, ruddy-skinned man was of Irish origin, but Jonathan had never admitted to such humble roots. His name was so conspicuously British that Wentworth suspected the family changed it at some point in order to assimilate.

He was tall, brawny, and had muscles upon muscles along with an appetite for unbridled sex that bordered on frightening. Yes indeed, this certainly could be the distraction he needed.

"Lieutenant, welcome." He moved around the chair and offered a hand. Jonathan's grip was firm, callused, and lingering.

Not taking his eyes from the watery-blue gaze, he said, "Smith, bring round a tray of tea and sandwiches. I am certain our guest is hungry after his journey."

He knew the well-mannered butler bowed before he heard the door close, but he did not see the gesture. All he saw were

Jonathan's greedy eyes almost stripping him with their sensual perusal.

"It has been a while, Jonathan." Wentworth slipped into their previous intimacy, now certain of Jonathan's reason for visiting.

"One year, six months, five days, and eighteen hours, *my* lord." The words were more a caress than an address, too casual to be polite, but then, considering what they both had in mind...

"Last time we met, I was Captain to you."

"Last time we met, we were on patrol around Portugal." He smiled slowly from one side of his mouth. "With a hundred other sailors nearby."

Wentworth returned the smile. "So, what brings you here today?"

"Simply passing through. I have business in Ashford, thought I'd give my solicitations."

"Good. Good indeed." Jonathan did not likely have business anywhere but here, but he would not bruise the man's pride by questioning his affairs.

A maid brought in a tray, and they busied themselves pouring tea and wine and devouring cold meat and cheese sandwiches. Men, especially horny men, had to eat, after all.

They discussed the navy and acquaintances they had in common. It was good to have someone with mutual interests with whom to chat. When the tray emptied and a light intoxication hummed through him, he strategically advanced the conversation.

"I was thinking, you have come at a good time. You must stay the night. I will have another place setting laid. Dine with me. Seems I am in need of distraction at the moment."

The younger man stiffened briefly, lips drawn in a slight

frown before shifting in his chair. Jonathan tilted his head down, his gaze half-visible behind tawny brows. "Thank you, my lord. I would indeed enjoy being with you. As it is, I have plenty of time."

The choice of words did not escape Wentworth's notice, nor did he miss the feral smile slipping into one of calculation.

❖

Later that day, and after they both changed for dinner, Wentworth could not remember what they ate as he walked into the study with his guest half a step behind.

Wentworth spent a portion of the meal staring over the table into Baker's familiar pale blue eyes. Eyes that were *not* brown. But Baker's eyes bordered on unpredictability, seductive but volatile. His temperament changed from moment to moment, and his ideas and purpose seemed to shift with mercurial fluidity. He had seen this part of Jonathan's personality before, and it had always been an aphrodisiac.

The other part of the meal he spent fending off Jonathan's foot, which toyed with his legs and, damnation, at one point his crotch. The lieutenant had always been bold, but in the privacy of Wentworth's mansion, he was positively brazen.

Walking to the sideboard and the glass decanters sitting there, Wentworth looked over his shoulder. "Port or whisky?"

He saw only the lieutenant's broad back as he closed and locked the door.

Shivers crawled up his spine.

The door secured now, they could do whatever they wanted in privacy. He'd not asked Jonathan to lock the door. Hector had done that task numerous times without being asked. So why did this event seem like a violation?

Knowing Jonathan's sexual appetites were not completely

wholesome had never bothered him because, his own sexual appetites were not wholesome either. Jonathan was an aggressive lover, sometimes bordering on cruel.

Wentworth could enjoy cruel right now; he needed the punishment. He could do what he wanted without worrying about emotions, stepping on toes, or being gentle. He could be as rough as he wanted and take out some of his frustration. In return, he would get back rough. Sometimes, he needed, craved rough. Sometimes the pain disciplined him for all his sins, made him forget his losses, and somehow made his sorry life and his bad deeds palatable.

Jonathan turned and stalked toward him, eyes half-lidded, one brow cocked with a promise of forbidden pleasures.

That look inflamed Wentworth's cock while it disturbed his soul. He lived to be in control. He was trained to be in control, but sometimes, in the early days of their relationship, Jonathan took that from him. The experience had been awkward, uncomfortable, salacious as an orgy in hell presided over by the devil himself. Was he ready to struggle for sexual supremacy? He certainly felt as though he needed punishment after abusing Hector, but…he was not quite certain.

"Neither port *nor* whisky. I want you."

Jonathan grabbed him at the nape of his neck and pulled him close. The kiss demanded Wentworth's attention with tongue and teeth. He had a moment of pain when Jonathan's tooth caught his lip, but then sheer sexual tension took over and he forgot the discomfort. This kiss he understood. It was a play for dominance.

And it tasted like duck and potatoes.

The kiss tasted like dinner, not like Will, not like Hector. In fact, it only tasted like food. Baker smelled of cologne, wool, and food. He had no distinct smell of his own. That alone made his erection flag.

Jonathan was the only man he knew who did not have his own smell. Rather peculiar. Scents were important. They created memories, connection, and desire, and he had none. His aroma changed depending on what he wore, what he ate, who did his laundry.

Funny he'd never noticed before.

Jonathan palmed the front of Wentworth's trousers and rubbed up and down, but Wentworth's member, only half-engaged, did not respond. What the hell was wrong? He'd satisfied his lust with Jonathan many times over the past five or so years when they were in the same port or, less often, when on the same ship.

Now, memories of tea-colored eyes ghosted across his mind. *Goddamn. What bloody lousy timing.* Now was the moment to fuck and nothing more. Nothing else was important right now. No complications, no attachments—just coupling, plain and simple.

He needed this physical distraction so he could overcome his grief and refocus his thinking.

The lieutenant laid an openmouthed kiss on him, practiced and near perfect as he pushed Wentworth's jacket down his arms, then pulled off the starched cravat. Without breaking the salt 'n' gravy kiss, he unbuttoned and removed Wentworth's shirt and then loosened the top button of his trousers because Wentworth could do nothing but stand there like an idiot.

Just stood there because he felt nothing. Absolutely nothing.

Trousers loose, Jonathan slipped a hand through the flap and grabbed Wentworth's cock. "Too much to drink?" he asked.

"I..."

Jonathan leaned in. "I live for challenges." He dived in for another kiss, teeth pinching against lips. The hand around his cock squeezed and yanked while his tongue thrust in, mimicking the act that should naturally follow. Rutting. Fucking.

Wentworth closed his eyes and endured the onslaught. He put his hands on the other man's shoulders for balance, not an embrace, but the lieutenant growled his pleasure as if the touch was a lover's caress.

The kiss was coarse, not playful and enticing like Hector's would be—back when he could still kiss him. He found himself wishing the hand on his cock was smaller, gentler, loving. Squeezing his eyes shut, he tried to pay attention to the friction. That would help, would it not?

He could do this. Wanted to do this. He'd shared pleasure with Jonathan many times in the past. Fifteen, maybe twenty times. It had always been pleasurable, if sometimes slightly painful. Their first time together, he even let Jonathan fuck him. He had to don soft cotton breeches for a few days after, but at the time, that had taken the edge off his lust and filled a base need. However, he had not allowed a repeat.

Jonathan growled again.

Opening his eyes, Wentworth saw his prick lying in Jonathan's brawny palm, looking for all the world like a dying snake.

"Want me to suck you instead, or do you need to bend over and let me take you?" Jonathan flexed his hips and shoved a properly engorged cock against Wentworth's thigh. "Think that could bring the limp member to attention?"

He pushed Jonathan away and half turned. Breathing deeply, he refastened his pants and walked to the fireplace, where he placed his forearm on the mantel and looked into the cold grate, suddenly wishing for a fire to warm the chill settling deep in his bones.

Impotence.

It had never happened to him before.

This night's endeavors proved that his own hand was better than empty, hollow sex. "This is not suitable for me at the moment."

"Suitable? Suitable! It is perfect. What are you talking about? Come, let me remind you how perfect it can be between us. We have always been perfect together," Jonathan purred in his deep baritone as one glistening bead of sweat rolled from his left temple to his granite-hard jaw. "It shall be ideal again. You'll see. Today, tomorrow, next week, months from now, we can have all this, and have it all the time."

Wentworth looked at the delicate gold clock on the mantel. It was ten thirty-six. He wondered why that seemed important. Now it was ten thirty-seven.

A gnawing in his gut that felt suspiciously like guilt came to the forefront of his attention. He felt as though he was being unfaithful to Hector. *That* was the problem. Why would he feel this way? This was not infidelity. They had exchanged no vows. They never even discussed anything past their fortnight together, let alone a commitment to mutual affections. Granted, Hector had professed wanting more. That sunny boy had even mentioned love.

Swallowing a lump in his throat, he reminded himself Hector had stormed out and left him. Sent no word he'd reached London safely. Wentworth had spent several days wondering and worrying until his men came back with Princess after delivering Hector's trunk. The sturdy horse arrived in fine form, so he had to assume Hector made the trip without mishap. Or at least made it *physically* unharmed.

His remorse grew as he considered what kind of harm to his spirits Hector had sustained at his hands.

Trying to control his emotions, he fought down the nagging shame that made his heart thump as though any moment Hector would walk through that study door and find him committing an act of infidelity. He had to place things in their proper perspective.

He found his perspective when he remembered his return to London three years prior.

❖

Autumn 1806, London

Will had changed, his agreeable temperament now impatient, hard, ruthless. His scar and limp more noticeable. Wentworth wanted nothing more than to scuttle the conversation, tired of listening to how the next bloody battle would do this, or win that, or kill so many. "Will, you are a man of science, a doctor. You're sworn to save lives, not inflict wounds and misery."

Will glared at him, tossed back his drink, and limped off through the dim, crowded ballroom to find gloomier company.

It would be easy to lose his temper and discard their long-standing friendship. But Wentworth's actions set events in motion that precipitated Will's downfall and his cavalier attitude toward life.

Some days, it seemed, Will possessed a desire to get himself killed.

Better pursue him before he started an altercation that led to a duel, but just then, he noticed a man with wide, luminous dark eyes glancing at him from the edge of the dance floor. He'd noticed the man and the glance a few times already, so he stared back. This time the gaze held. The young man was beautiful, and Wentworth knew him, but damnation, had he improved with age.

All thoughts of Will vanished as Wentworth made his way

across the dance floor, under the flickering chandeliers, no easy feat in such a crush, to reacquaint himself with the man with those beautiful eyes.

Hector Somerville was no longer a lad.

❖

At the time, he had felt guilty over his attraction to Hector after so many years of devotion to Will.

Ironic that now he felt shame for kissing another man, when he'd been unable to make himself kiss Hector. He would get Hector back once he determined how to achieve such a lofty goal.

Jonathan was uncharacteristically quiet and still.

Perhaps it was the void of activity that dragged Wentworth back to the present.

Jonathan stood in the middle of the room, straight and strong, a few years younger than Wentworth. He was handsome and all male, with no-nonsense thin lips and a broad nose and jaw. But instead of fucking, he stood here flat-cocked, remembering a party and large brown eyes.

Ridiculous, considering his lust the first time he'd seen Jonathan, who'd been laughing, head thrown back, light mane falling across his shoulders while standing on the deck of the HBMS *Juno*. Amused at another crewman's joke, he personified masculine beauty. Wentworth had been unable to do anything but stare. When Jonathan noticed him, lust sparked between them. Wentworth had known they would be together that night.

That was the first time Wentworth had done some of the things two men could do together. He walked a little crooked for a week and suspected the lieutenant, a midshipman back then, was forced to put his breeches on slowly and gently for a few days after.

But there was nothing now—no interest, no lust, nothing. Why was this the first time he noticed emptiness in those pale eyes? As if the sea and sun had sucked away all sense of moral decency from the darkened, temperamental mind that lurked behind them. Baker did not seem quite stable.

Within a few hours of their reassociation, Wentworth decided it would be best to keep him at arm's length.

Chapter Twelve

"It's the Somerville milksop, isn't it?" Something sparked in those sea-spray eyes.

Diplomacy would work best in this situation, but Wentworth truly felt like striking out at Jonathan. He wanted to inflict pain so that he was not the only miserable one. Instead, he went for something in between. "Perhaps you should leave tomorrow. Go on about your business. It would not do for you to linger here when you have important tasks to attend to."

"It is him, isn't it?"

"Him?"

"That sniveling little brat I saw you leave Somerville's house with. Horatio or whatever his name is."

Wentworth narrowed his eyes in warning. "What do you know of that?"

"I attended the christening. I know the Somervilles, so of course I went to pay my respects. Imagine my surprise to see you pull up, knowing your history with the family."

Wentworth's blood started to boil. No one knew his history with the family. How did this man find out?

"He is too young, too immature for you," Jonathan said. "He has done nothing with his life as far as I can tell. You deserve…You *need* a real man." He stood there, hands on hips and muscles flexing.

"Hector Somerville is none of your concern. I suggest you drop the topic."

High color inflamed his face. Shoulders tense, feet spread shoulder width apart, he'd buckled down, preparing for a fight.

Wentworth wanted none of that, so he changed the subject to mundane things. Eventually, his stiff demeanor eased, but when Wentworth suggested playing a game of chess, Jonathan declined.

The next day the lieutenant was gone.

❖

Wentworth poured himself another brandy and watched the flames hungrily consume wood. He took a sip, but the smooth oaky taste did not blunt the dragon's teeth gnawing on his gut.

He watched the flames as he folded the paper again and again, pressing the seams tightly and cleanly as he had been taught years ago.

Despite the warm evening and the sweat running between his shoulder blades, the fire was not yet hot enough for what he intended. It required another log. He rose, limbs stiff from an hour's inactivity. Jonathan had been gone and forgotten for two weeks, yet the man was paramount in his thoughts today.

He addressed Gabriel's portrait. "I really would like some suggestion as to how to proceed. This is new territory for me, brother."

After placing a very large log on the flames, he poured his third brandy. He planned on getting drunk enough to numb the dragon's bite.

He took a swallow.

Finally, the fire boiled with heat.

He finished the last few seams. Creasing the paper, he remembered performing these movements before, only before his motions were guided by dark, callused, knowledgeable fingers.

This time he folded alone.

In the end, he had to scrape off a bit of cheap wax that at one time sealed the missive, which arrived in the day's post. The irony lay in the fact that when he received the letter, his trunks were already packed for his trip to London—he'd planned to leave early and try once more to convince Hector they could work things out. Only an hour ago, the letter arrived and changed everything, yet for some reason, he could not stop thinking about one spectacular evening.

❖

Autumn 1806, London

The dinner party at Wentworth's town house had been a success. With the late hour the guests were gone, except for Hector. They sipped their port in the dark, candlelit study, both having loosened their cravats and unbuttoned a few buttons.

"Refill?" Hector asked, walking toward Wentworth's chair. Hell, his crotch was at eye level, and Wentworth could see which way he dressed.

Then he rested his hand on Wentworth's shoulder, seemingly with camaraderie. He gripped Hector's masculine hand—a strong hand, rough and calloused—and a surge of sensual energy zipped through Wentworth's every pore. He might have moaned. Unlikely, but it was possible.

Over the past few weeks since their reintroduction at the party, they had managed to find similar events in which they shared an interest, and every time they met, one or both of them had made sure to brush against the other or share a brief touch.

He did not imagine the attraction. Hector shared his interest.

Wentworth would play the role of seducer tonight but would need to go gently. Hector had such an air of innocence, Wentworth was convinced he'd never been with a man before. He exhibited too much nervousness and shyness to have any experience.

Raising Hector's exquisite hand to his mouth, he placed one gentle kiss on his palm. The skin smelled wonderful, sunshine and male, not perfumed and insipid like so many fops he knew.

Hector inhaled a slow, wavering breath, closed his eyes, and leaned against the chair for support. His erection touched Wentworth's arm. An accident, for certain, because Hector pulled away at once, but not before Wentworth sported an answering cock stand.

He pulled at Hector's hand and urged him to walk to the front of the chair. Hands still entwined, staring into his eyes, heart pounding, he pulled Hector slowly down for a soft, sweet kiss. Lips only, no teeth.

The smell of arousal hit his senses, along with starch and sweat. "God...heaven."

It was so unlike him to lose his reserved sarcasm, but with heart racing, his nerves on fire, wondering if this were real or a dream, he leaned back. He was afraid to break contact in case the dream evaporated like a land mirage at sea, while at the same time he assessed the real risk of someone walking in on them. "Lock the door, Hector."

The young man broke contact immediately, as if burned.

Would he run now that he'd come to his senses? Would he leave and never return?

Hector shook himself, as if the sensations were too intense. Looking at the floor, he walked to the door and hesitated. He reached for the knob, pressing his head against the wood, rolling it side to side.

Had the boy decided to leave? Would there be no seduction? Wentworth stood, unsure what to do. "Hector?" His voice was an octave lower than planned, choked with regret, desire.

Hector turned slowly and looked him up, then down. "God, you're perfect." He swallowed audibly. He almost took a step toward Wentworth. Almost, but then he put his foot back in place.

When Hector didn't move, Wentworth raised one hand, palm up. He would not force him to decide—since this certainly was his first time—but he would encourage him to decide in favor of pleasure, desire, and companionship.

Before he had a chance to speak, Hector locked the door, sealing their fate.

Hector went to him, mouth slightly open, pulse jumping in his throat.

Taking the last step to bring them together, Wentworth drank in his radiant gaze, the lustful expression, the trust. *He rubbed his thumb across the side of Hector's firm, wide mouth.*

What a sight. His shaking thumb on that beautiful, irresistible mouth. His heart jumped around in his chest and his whole body trembled. He lowered his head—God and the devil couldn't have stopped him at this point—and kissed soft lips.

Holy Mother, he was inflamed. He trailed a touch along a firm back to an equally firm arse, and slowly, as if taming a wild animal, brought their crotches together. Hector flexed his hips, sending the most enjoyable friction against his cock. He sucked in a breath, ready to come, just like that. How embarrassing.

"*We must slow down, my lusty young man.*" *He backed off and laughed.* "*There is much better yet to come than a quick rut, fully clothed.*"

Taking Hector's hand, he rubbed it along the front of his breeches. At the exquisite pressure, he gritted his teeth, put his head back, and gasped for breath. He might not be able to last for "*more to come.*"

Backing away from the fine touch, he led Hector to the carpet near the fireplace. Not caring about ruining his own tailored clothing, he reclined on the lush carpet and once again raised a beckoning hand.

Hector swallowed, took the offering, and with shy, slow movements lay down next to Wentworth as though he were about to lie next to sin itself. He sat with one leg under his arse, the other crooked in his circled arm. Committed, perhaps, but not completely.

Wentworth smiled. Good. Committed is enough for now. I can convince him. *Leaning forward, he touched Hector's cheek. Dark evening stubble marred the smooth skin underneath. He stared into eyes turned black in the dimly lit room. Hector's muscles were tense, quivering ever so slightly under Wentworth's touch.* "*Hector, my dear, we can stop at any time. You realize, do you not?*"

Nodding, he pressed his cheek into Wentworth's hand, and that meant there would be no stopping.

With his heart thumping triple time, he touched his lips to Hector's. They were warm, firm.

He ran his tongue along Hector's perfect lips, enticing them open before he drove in. Gasping, he inhaled Hector's scent. Fresh and clean like the outdoors, the country...No, not quite right. More like spring. His breath momentarily transported Wentworth to a sun-warmed glade where the two of them sat in lush grass, kissing and touching.

Hector moved into the kiss, and Wentworth snapped back to the study. He pulled away—almost, but not truly, startled. Fire warmed his back, and Hector looked half debauched already—his eyes closed, mouth open, leaning even farther until Wentworth closed the gap and kissed the lovely lad again.

He lay Hector upon the carpet and brought their chests together.

Sighing, Hector seized his shoulders and tentatively tasted Wentworth's mouth.

With a surge of near giddiness he had not felt in years, Wentworth sucked on Hector's invading tongue and ran his hand along his chest, abdomen, thigh, and then, with his fingertips, he sampled the size of Hector's cock stand.

Hector arched off the floor.

Unable to resist such a long, hard, eager cock, Wentworth rubbed his hand along the cloth-covered shaft. "Hector. God, I need you. Right now, need..." He bit the side of his cheek hard and shoved his own erection against the floor to slow his imminent climax. After several shallow breaths, he continued. "*I will remove your trousers. Is this acceptable?*"

Hector nodded frantically and kicked off his shoes, then lifted his arse so Wentworth could divest him of trousers and smalls. They even took the time to remove his socks.

Good God, Hector was spectacular—lean, sculpted muscles, sparse body hair, and a long, jutting cock leaking at the tip. Nearly drooling for a taste of that prick, Wentworth closed his eyes and slowed his breathing. He would not scare Hector. He would take this slowly. "*I plan to touch you...with my hand and then my mouth. Will you allow this attention?*"

With wide-open eyes, Hector opened his mouth, closed it, then nodded.

Damn, when had Hector lost his tongue? Not a visit went by without his delightful digressions. Now he had no words at all.

Wentworth chuckled, and to buy himself time to put his desire on simmer instead of fast boil, he stood and slowly removed his clothing. Hector watched every move of his hand, every slip of clothing until those guileless eyes fastened on Wentworth's raging stand. He swallowed audibly and finally found his tongue. "May...May I...touch..." He looked into Wentworth's eyes, his expression one of pure amazement. "I want you to do everything you just mentioned, and I want to do them to you as well."

Wentworth shivered at the thought of the young man's hands and mouth all over his body. "Take off the rest of your clothing, my dear. We have important things to get to."

Within moments, they were both stripped to bare skin, and Wentworth lay atop him. Kissing that sweet, sweet mouth, he flexed his hips and rubbed his cock against Hector's. The lad stopped kissing, mouth lax and body arching up to meet Wentworth's assault.

Wentworth pulled off—too close—and he realized Hector was only seconds away from climax. Afraid there was no stopping the desire set in motion, he set his mouth and fist to work on the virgin's member, and seconds later had the satisfying tang of spend in his mouth and the ecstatic writhing of rapture beneath him.

And then Hector's reticence broke. "Oh God. Oh, my mother and God and of all...Now...Now...Yes...you are spectacular. I...I...May we do that again? God, yes. So good. I must say that was the most...Mmm! Yes. Yes. Wentworth!"

Hector opened his eyes, still writhing, and speared Wentworth with a sleepy, wanton gaze. "I want more."

Wentworth's heart nearly burst with delight. Never had he relished such a pleasure in his bed—well, floor actually, but same thing.

"We can do anything you wish. Would you like me to fuck you?"

"Oh God." Hector choked, coughed, and cleared his throat. "Yes. Now? Is it possible to do it now? Here? On the floor?"

"My dear, it is very possible that we will indeed do so." He grabbed the sleeve of his coat splayed on the floor a few feet to the right and dragged it to them. He had come prepared for their after-dinner port, knowing any disruption from his seduction might scare Hector away. He plucked the ampule of unscented oil from the coat pocket and popped the cork. Spreading oil on his prick and slicking his fingers, he reclined over Hector's trembling body and kissed those expressive lips. Hector levered himself from the floor to meet him inch for inch, wrapping strong fingers around Wentworth's neck, keeping them pinned together.

"Have you ever?" Wentworth knew the answer as his oil-slicked fingers touched Hector's entrance.

The man jumped and slowly shook his head. "Never wanted to. Not enough to…well, take the risk."

"You want it now," Wentworth said as he slid one digit into Hector's tight hole.

Hector whispered, "More than breath itself."

And that was good. So very, very good. Because he could not have stopped himself if his own life stood in the balance.

"My dear. My sweet, sweet dear." He slipped in a second finger, and Hector clamped then released.

"Wentworth. I love…love y— This. I love this."

The tightening clench around Wentworth's chest was nearly suffocating. "Me as well, dear, dear Hector."

Unsure where these strange, overwhelming emotions stemmed from, Wentworth used action to cover his sudden trepidation. He pushed in another finger and then another, Hector's muscles again tightening and releasing with each invasion. He crooked his fingers to find the spot that would release Hector's tension, and when he hit the target, his lover arched up and shouted.

"Wentworth. Fuck me. Goddamn, now. Fuck me into the floor. I need…need something. Help me." He punched the floor with his balled fists.

And Wentworth gave him what he wanted. Gently pulling out of Hector's body, he used his slick hand to guide his cock to Hector's stretched entrance and pushed just a little, giving him time to change his mind. He did not. In fact, he pushed against the invading cock until the head began to slip inside.

Wentworth pushed Hector to the floor with a hand to his stomach. "Wait, you really must go slowly, or the first time will be painful."

Dark eyes watched his every word, his every move.

"I need something, and I cannot wait. Do something now, or I fear I might perish."

Wentworth chuckled and pushed against the tight circle of muscles. "You, my dear one, will survive. Of that I am certain." He pushed again, and this time the head of his cock slipped past the ring of tight muscle.

Hector gasped, and a torrent of prickly desire surged through Wentworth's body to the point he could no longer think. He rushed forward, and Hector cried out. He forced himself to stop, and it was the most difficult thing he had ever done. "Hector. I'm so sorry. Are you hurt? Damn, I hurt you."

Hector lay on his back, panting.

Damnation, he should have known he was too inept to take a virgin. Heavens knew the one and only other time had been a near disaster, so why did he feel competent to do so now?

"Relax, and I will slip out carefully. We do not have to continue."

But Hector reared up, clasping Wentworth's arse cheeks as he did so, and seated himself on Wentworth's rod.

"Jesus." Wentworth felt the contractions that speeded the end of this union, and fought for control. He wanted, no, needed to guide Hector to a pleasurable first fuck. Five deep breaths and a severe self-scolding had him in control.

Hector panted beneath him in what looked like either painful pleasure or pleasurable pain.

Wentworth flexed his hips, and Hector opened his eyes and lifted toward him. Wentworth's heart lightened, and he started moving. "So warm, so tight. Damnation, you are beautiful. So…" His thoughts left him, his words gone. All that remained was the warm, loving body below him and the young man's moans of pleasure.

Hector came in a whirlwind of cries, come, and caresses of Wentworth's back and arse. This pushed Wentworth over the edge, and he spilled into the man's virgin arse with the spangle of raw nerves and new pleasure. When the shock wave running through his body calmed, he collapsed upon his lover.

Hector gathered him close and kissed his forehead. "Had I known it would be this monumental, I would not have waited so long."

Pain shot through Wentworth's heart, and he growled.

When Hector laughed, Wentworth growled again, louder, and Hector said, "What I meant to say is, I would have approached you sooner."

"Good man, Hector. Good man." And Wentworth did not want to know why he was so concerned with Hector's declaration. After all, Wentworth had had many lovers in the past.

"Wentworth?"

"Hmm."

"I feel somewhat squashed. Do you—"

Immediately, Wentworth rolled him over to lie against his chest. "This better?"

Hector laid his head on Wentworth's torso and sighed. "This is perfect." And Wentworth agreed. Perfection in his arms, in his study, and on his luxurious carpet. He had waited for this his entire life without ever realizing.

❖

Crack!

A large log broke in the grate, dragging Wentworth's gaze off a dark wax smudge on the paper dragon. The burnt orange smear made the *zhezhi* animal appear fierce.

Amazing he still remembered how to make the folds and creases required to form a shape after so many years. He was not amazed he remembered the Chinese captain who taught him how to make the tiny ornament. They had not understood a word of each other's language, but they understood each other's passion, a shared desire, an appetite that almost ignited two countries.

He walked over, rubbing dampness from his checks, and singeing the hair on his hand, placed the little dragon on top of the roiling flames. He watched the little animal ignite, watched the painful secrets hidden within turn to smoke.

Chapter Thirteen

Spring 1809, London

There was a commotion in the entryway. Wentworth left the library to see what was amiss. He arrived in time to see Will arguing with Smith.

"William!"

The two men jumped apart and faced him, expressions mutinous.

"Smith, do let the man in."

Both men straightened their jackets in quick, tight movements.

"Well, come, then." He gestured to the library, and Will followed.

"I must say, it is unusual for Smith to confront visitors. What did you say to the old fellow?"

Will shoved his fists in his pockets and leaned a shoulder against a mahogany bookshelf. His face radiated disgust bordering on hatred. He shrugged. "Perhaps he took exception to my impatience. I rushed in insisting on seeing you immediately without being introduced."

"Did you think I would refuse you?"

Will shrugged again. "I couldn't take that risk. I need to know what you've done to Hector."

Wentworth's blood froze in his veins. He knew the letter he received two days ago, full of hate and accusations, was an ill omen. If Hector was hurt... He sat down hard on the edge of his desk, slipped off, caught himself, and sat again. He could barely take in a breath, his chest squeezed his lungs so forcefully. "What happened?"

"I hoped you would know. He's been avoiding me. But I finally found him entering his lodgings. I have never seen him so down and unresponsive."

His blood flowed once more. Hector was unhurt. Upset for a certainty, but no lasting damage, which had been a possibility given the anger and hatred in the letter he'd burned.

"You remember, he's always been a happy, resilient boy. I've only seen him like this one other time."

Wentworth turned to his desk, trying to block out the words, not wanting to hear the rest of what Will had to say. He already had enough guilt in his soul to drown ten men.

"He's been moody since your fortnight together, but it's getting worse, not better with time. What happened to him in Kent? What did you do to him?"

Pursing his lips in disgust, Wentworth again thought of that hateful letter. Upon receiving it, he'd rushed to London, and then...he had hesitated. His plan had been to run over, grab Hector, and kiss him. Force him to let go of the anger and come back to him. Instead, he'd struggled with that plan until it was too late to make a call. And now he was still hesitating.

So he bared his soul to Will, which was remarkably easy to do. The man he had loved for years, his best friend since they were children. He had missed being able to share confidences these past few years. "I was a prick during our sojourn in Kent, I will confess. I could not give him what he wanted." He turned to Will, who looked about ready to ignite. "Hear me out, Will, please."

He took a deep breath and continued. "I wrote him several times, trying to apologize, to set things right. I went by his rooms, but he refused to see me. Apparently, I did a spectacular job of pushing him away while we were in Kent. We were good together, but I could not let go of the past, could not tell him the truth. When the truth came to light, I did not handle the situation with grace and patience. I believe I may have slowly and completely killed his vibrancy." Bloody hell! His insides hurt, cramped, and he thought he might cry for the first time in over a decade.

Will clenched his fists. "You worthless, bloody—"

"You don't have to tell me what you think of my behavior. Rest assured, I am harder on myself than anyone else could ever be." God knew he had fretted over his actions ever since receiving the missive.

"Just tell me what you did."

"I told him about us."

Will spun around, shoulders hunched, fists clenched. "Damn. You are intent on self-destruction, aren't you? It's a wonder he didn't pull down one of your rapiers and run you through and then come after me with it. Why?"

"I had to tell him. I got myself in a situation...Well, I had to tell him or lie as boldly as a member of the House of Commons the eve before election."

"Bloody hell, Ty."

"Don't judge me any further, Will. The issue here is not me and my unnatural tastes, it's Hector's health. As I said, I came to London to set the matter straight. It's just..." Taking another deep breath, he ignored the feeling of inadequacy. "I put off calling on him as I can't figure out exactly what to say, and I am not certain Hector will even talk to me at this point."

"I see." Will paced the room, his anger evident in each

aggressive step. "Here is what you will do. Leave Hector alone, don't see him again. I shall talk with my brother and demand he get over your poor treatment. Between me and Mary, we shall set Hector back on the right track and get him over all his mistaken allegiances." He turned and glared. "Go back to Kent, Ty. Your presence here will not help this matter." With that declaration, he turned on his heel and stormed from the room.

As soon as he heard the front door slam, Wentworth called for his carriage.

❖

Wentworth licked his lips for the second time in as many minutes. They were still dry, but he stopped himself before performing the annoying action a third time. He did not want to make a habit of acting like a nervous debutante.

After glancing at the cobbles for horse dung, he stepped out of his carriage into the glaring afternoon sun, then passed the footman announcing his presence.

The gray-haired housekeeper who answered the door bobbled her head incessantly and wrung her hands as she curtsied. "Please, my lord. Just a moment while I off and check to see if the master is at 'ome to ye."

She allowed him to enter the first of the set of rooms. Nothing had changed since his last visit. They were compact and no-nonsense, so unlike their tenant. Hector was so bold and beautiful that the rooms always seemed drab by comparison. Light brown and green walls, small carpets, a handful of uninspired landscapes.

The housekeeper was new, but the lodgings were as familiar to him as his own skin, even though more than two bloody long years had passed since he'd been allowed through the front door.

The gray-haired woman returned with a wide smile, no longer wringing her hands, but she still bobbled. "My lord, the master will see ye. If ye will come this way, he will be right along. I'll bring a tray, and Lieutenant Baker will entertain ye while ye wait."

He stopped dead in his tracks. *Jonathan is here? With Hector? Whatever the hell for?*

Damnation.

He knew Jonathan and Hector were together. The letter he received from Jonathan two days ago had said as much, but he had assumed it was for a night, two at the most. He had convinced himself Hector was smart enough to choose a better man than himself next time, and then Red Jon was here this early in the morning, as if he had stayed the night.

He licked his lips again.

Bloody. Hell.

He walked down the wide hallway to Hector's large study, just to freeze again as memories seized his muscles. They were having a picnic in December on the carpet in front of the fireplace, feeding Hector out-of-season grapes, kissing him slowly, teasingly. Making love to him. At the time it was fucking, not lovemaking. Just fucking. Oh, but the fucking had been more potent than a nor'easter. More beautiful than St. Elmo's fire. More—well, more meaningful to him than he'd realized.

His chest ached at the memory of Hector beneath him. The *perfection* of Hector beneath him, his wide, luminous eyes looking up at him. Not trying to hide. Open. Facing their liaison with complete participation and anticipation.

The naïve young fool.

Yet he could not suppress the grin as he continued into the warm marigold and hunter-green study.

"Glad to see you in good spirits and as elegant as usual, Wentworth."

Jonathan.

The grin fell from Wentworth's face faster than water plummets off a cliff. What the hell *was* Hector doing with him? Still the dreamer, hooking up with someone so wholly unworthy.

He reached up to rub an aching throb in his chest but stopped before hand touched silk. He could not show weakness just now.

Jonathan, big, strong, and golden, gestured him into an armchair across from where he sprawled with rawboned ease in an impeccable dark olive morning suit.

No. He definitely could not show weakness. He would help Hector, who obviously needed the intervention of a mature, knowledgeable man who had seen more of the world's snares and knew Jonathan's manipulative nature firsthand.

Relying on training and years of experience leading a crew, he hardened his features and showed no fear. "Jonathan, I am surprised to see you here. Still sniffing around blood too blue for the likes of you?"

Jonathan's lips thinned, but his smile held. "I have been here a very long time. Many months. The better part of a year, in fact," he said with the overly formal speech of someone born poor but who had worked his way up the ranks with claws and determination.

Normally, Wentworth admired that tenacity. Not today.

Better part of a year? So Hector began dallying with Jonathan shortly after leaving Kent? That meant he'd been with Jonathan while Wentworth had been groveling in letters and prostrating himself at Hector's door, seeking admittance, trying to convince him another chance might be all they needed to get it right? And all that time Hector had been with Jonathan, who spun manipulations like spiderwebs.

How much of his humiliation had Jonathan witnessed?

"So, after some time with Hector, you came to see me," Wentworth said. *Why?* "Does he know of your visit?"

"Men have needs."

Damn it all. He had always hated Jonathan's games. Playing along and hoping he chose the most irritating reply, he said, "Yes, well, by all means, go back off to sea so you no longer have to suffer tedious months in London."

Jonathan threw back his head and laughed. "Oh, Wentworth, that is what I always adored about you—you never mince words. Get right to the thick of things."

"Unlike you, Lieutenant. One never knows where they stand with you, do they? You would just as easily embrace a man as stab him in the back."

Jonathan looked away, but his smile remained. "Brandy?"

Wentworth sat properly in the nearest chair, not sprawled like some ruffian. It was never a good idea to drop one's guard when in the presence of the enemy. "What are your objectives here, Jonathan?"

The toad laughed again. An annoying, fully in-control-of-the-situation laugh.

Wentworth fought the urge to jump up. He did not want to sit here exchanging barbs. He wanted to fight.

Wentworth bit back a snarl. "If you so much as hurt one of Hector's fingers, I swear—"

"What? You realize you hurt him more than I ever possibly could? You almost crippled the boy with your high-minded ideas and self-righteous rigor."

Jonathan's observation was so close to the mark, Wentworth would have been dead if words were cannon balls. As it was, he only bled regret.

Hector then strode into the room and stood behind Jonathan's chair.

"Lord Wentworth," Hector said. His voice was deep and warm, but the formality of address after all they had shared nearly sliced him in two. Jonathan reached up to take Hector's hand, then placed it on his shoulder, both hands still clasped in a show of solidarity.

That hollow ache rose in Wentworth's chest again. What more did he deserve, really?

"I'm aware the two of you are acquainted," Hector said, but his focus landed somewhere around Wentworth's left shoulder. "So, let us not dance around the topic. What, or who, are you here for?"

The indifference and distance in those previously guileless, trusting, loving eyes was such a crime. Worse yet, Wentworth knew the blame lay solely at his feet.

Chapter Fourteen

Hector tried not to grimace at the too-tight squeeze Jonathan gave his hand. He attempted to control everything, to be sure, but he was awfully smug today in front of Wentworth, like he'd won the Ascot with Hector the prize gelding.

"You should know, I offered to have a committed relationship with Hector," Jonathan said. He lifted Hector's hand, then pulled him onto his lap. Hector allowed it but felt stupid and insignificant, no longer in control of his life.

Wentworth's face twitched, and he half rose from the chair.

What is he thinking? Hector wondered. Never easy to tell with that stoic man. Although knowing Wentworth, he was probably incensed, and his next comment confirmed that.

"You know this man!" He waved somewhere around the chair he and Jonathan sat in. "You must know he is not to be trusted. Besides, two men cannot commit. There are no laws, no rules to allow such a thing." He rose the rest of the way out of his chair and rubbed his hand across his chest, like he'd been smacked with a mallet.

Hector felt the anger spill over him, so he said something he really didn't mean. "Sometimes it only takes a short while with the right person. One day you wake up and you are certain. I imagine this is something you don't know about, isn't that right, Wentworth?" he asked, hackles rising the way only Wentworth could make them prickle.

"I know." He whispered the word to the ground. At that moment, with shoulders drooping and creases around his eyes and forehead, Wentworth looked twenty years older, bitter, lost.

But Hector would not feel sympathy for a man who could have had anything—*everything*—from him but refused to accept the gift.

He struggled out of Jonathan's clutches. Carefully, avoiding the word *love*, Hector said, "I want commitment." But he had not accepted Jonathan's offer. Not yet, anyway. And why not? What was he waiting for?

He had adored the attention at first, having someone who treated him like a prized possession. But the possessiveness started to strangle within a few months, and he began to notice the sideways compliments.

He wasn't certain he wanted to accept Jonathan's offer, but he was still well aware Wentworth had never offered anything. "You could not propose what I most cherished."

Wentworth finally looked up. "I could…You should…" He left the last unsaid as he reached a hand out as if to touch Hector. Wentworth looked at Jonathan and then back. "May I speak with you alone for a few moments?"

Hector shook his head. That was not a sound idea, but he didn't have to say as much. Jonathan took the situation out of his hands by lurching out of his lazy recline and going for Wentworth, shoving Hector out of the way.

Hector shouted in surprise, "Stop, Jonathan."

Wentworth did not back away, even with fifteen stone of wild-eyed Irish muscle crowding him.

"I suggest you leave now, *Lord Wentworth*, before my lover asks me to rearrange your pretty features for you."

"Do consider, accomplishing that feat may not be as easy as you believe, Jonathan."

Had these been two men Hector did not know, if it were happening on the street and not in his house, he could have enjoyed watching two finely formed men, one dark and one light, displaying. As it was, he was afraid this would escalate until someone was badly hurt or killed. He must stop them.

He pushed them apart and forced his voice to be calm and commanding, like Wentworth's. "Gentlemen, stop at once. Jonathan, go pour some port or something."

Jonathan looked at him as if he had just suggested he knit a scarf, but he did back a few feet away.

"And, Wentworth, it is time you leave. You were not invited, and you have greatly outstayed your welcome."

"Hector, I—"

"Leave, Wentworth. I do not wish to see you."

"If you would just hear me out."

"There is nothing to hear, *my lord.* You had all the chances you deserve and then some. I will listen to you no longer."

"There are many things I need for you to hear. Things that will explain—"

Hector lost his temper. "I have had all the half-truths and misperceptions from you that I ever intend to accept." He flung his hand up and pointed. "Leave my home now."

The muscles in Wentworth's face jumped and trembled. "I—"

Hector pointed to the exit again, this time with greater emphasis, and said under his breath so only he and Wentworth could hear, "You slept with my brother and never told me. Hell, you were in love with him when you seduced me. Perhaps you still are."

Wentworth hesitated, closed his eyes and swallowed, and shook his head slowly. He whispered, "I am sorry. So terribly sorry." And then he turned and left the room. A moment later, the front door clicked shut.

❖

Wentworth jammed the light gray top hat on his head and stormed toward Hyde Park. The impact of his thick leather heels on the cobbles rattled his teeth despite his clenched jaw. Too agitated to take his carriage, he walked home. Hell, he was too agitated to walk, moving at a pace closer to a run.

What the hell had he been thinking? Showing up unannounced. Of all the damnable…

What had he expected to accomplish by coming here in the first place? Damn fool. He had convinced himself that if he just popped in, Hector would relish the chance to take up where they left off without a backward glance. Finding Jonathan there had been like stepping off a cliff only to land on a shale shelf ten feet below and having the air knocked out of his lungs.

I am without a doubt the most arrogant, self-righteous idiot to ever walk London's streets.

Images filled his mind of the things Jonathan had no doubt done to Hector. Things he *would* do. Hell, perhaps he was doing some of them currently.

He stopped dead in his tracks. Looking around at all the happy couples, he wondered if he could scream and wave his fists in the air without being hauled off as a madman. Likely not, so he channeled his loathing and pain into a pounding walk. He would scream when he reached his study.

What could be done? Hector was an adult and had made up his mind. God, he had looked spectacular in his indignant anger. All grown up and decisive. Passionate. Gorgeous…and way beyond his reach.

Sometime in the past year, Hector had turned into a man. Or was it that Wentworth finally realized he was a man?

For a few brief moments, he'd considered fighting over Hector, taking all his frustration out on Jonathan, but even if they'd fought and Wentworth had won, the matter of who Hector chose was out of his control. The only thing that kept him from throwing the first blow was that Jonathan already looked like the hero in that setting.

And Wentworth looked like a villain.

Jamming his hands deep into his pockets, he picked up his pace. The sooner he arrived at his town house, the sooner he could get on with his plan to drink himself into numbness.

❖

Hector stared at the spot where only moments ago Wentworth had reached out to him. He felt the tingle of indignation flow away, diluted with something that would feel like sadness if it didn't hurt so horribly.

He didn't have time to think about Wentworth, however, because Jonathan stood nearby. Jonathan, who was always around these days. Jonathan, who touched his shoulder and turned him around.

Hector looked at his broad, green-covered chest, to be precise. At the moment, he couldn't stomach the gloating expression he knew would be on his face.

With a murmur, warm and deep as a bubbling pot of oxtail soup, Jonathan said, "You see, he doesn't love you. Not like I do. I can overlook your flaws, your imperfections." Jonathan ran a sweaty finger over one of Hector's odd eyebrows.

He'd never realized his eyebrows were odd until Jonathan commented on them. He'd never realized his hair was too ordinary, either, or that he was too slim and too quiet. Too quiet? Him, quiet? Only around Jonathan, who found fault with everything he said. The touch gave Hector a cold shiver. Not a warm shiver like Wentworth used to elicit.

Oh God, the shivers Wentworth could elicit…

❖

Something was wrong. Definitely wrong.

Jon glared through Hector's mullioned study window at Hector. He'd been acting off the past few months. Distracted. No, not distracted—distant. Even before Wentworth's untimely visit that morning, Hector was losing interest, and his dissatisfaction grew by the day. That was why Jon had been to see Wentworth. Stirring up trouble between those two would only remind Hector how much he hated Wentworth and would keep him away.

Hector, the young romantic, meandered through the roses in the small park across the street. To a casual observer, he simply appeared to be enjoying the late afternoon sunshine. Jon knew better. He knew he was losing Hector. Their liaison had been intense, but now his affection was waning. He was certain Hector contemplated how to politely break from this alliance. No commitment between the two of them, no snubbing Wentworth where it would hurt most, no keeping them apart.

He was losing.

He would lose the gambit and his aristocrat. Again.

Grabbing a snifter from a small table, he squeezed it instead of punching a fist through the glass panes.

Hector wouldn't stay with him much longer. All his plans, his hard work, and his wasted attentions ruined because of Wentworth's untimely visit.

No. He refused to lose the gambit.

Crystal shattered with a shrill snap and tinkle before he registered throwing the snifter across the room.

Outside, Hector looked up and then at the window. He must have heard the breaking glass. Jon smiled. Hector lifted one side of his mouth. That was all, nothing more, before going back to studying the flower beds.

Jon tapped a staccato on the window casing. It was time for drastic action. He would not let Hector go back to Wentworth.

He had lost the viscount, whom he'd set his hat for from the first time they'd come together, but he'd always been out of reach. Despite all his enticement, Wentworth never spent more than a few hours at a time with him. The arrogant bastard.

Dark thoughts kept Jon company these days, feeding him. An angry hatred gnawed at his gut, keeping him strong and smart. He would obliterate Wentworth's conceit. After all, Hector was still his, and he would find a way to keep him from anyone else.

Jon turned and trod out of the room, pulverizing shards of crystal underfoot as he went.

CHAPTER FIFTEEN

Hector choked on the rotten fish and garbage stench of the Thames as the carriage approached the wharf. Ship masts towered behind warehouses and other buildings.

This was a *monumentally* bad idea. Why had he let Jonathan talk him into an outing, especially such an ill-conceived one as this?

Outside their hired hackney, the wharf teemed with people—mostly men, but with a handful of tough-looking women in the mix. Everyone seemed in a hurry, most of them carrying large loads of goods. He looked across the sea of humanity to the ships. There was frantic activity on board as well.

Half-dressed men climbed masts and did…What was it exactly they all did? Tying sails, untying ropes and resecuring them someplace else. It was all a mystery to him, though his past two companions had an intimate knowledge of everything nautical. Why had he not taken the time to learn something about their profession?

After Wentworth's visit yesterday, he had finally made a decision. It should not have been so difficult but took him a sleepless night nonetheless. It was so unlike him to take this long to decide which direction he should go, but his liaison with Jonathan was obviously headed toward disaster. He would not commit to a man he didn't trust. Hell, he didn't even like him. He would let him know today so they could both stop this charade.

Honestly, it wasn't even a pleasure to be around him anymore. He'd be alone for a while, or who knew, maybe forever, but that was preferable to being unhappy with an ill-tempered, ill-bred, ill-mannered man for whom he had slowly lost all affection.

So, why had he let Jonathan convince him—no, it was more like coerce him—into coming here today? Here of all places. He needed to grow a backbone and stop letting people walk all over him. He would start that as soon as he was gone from this disagreeably loud, smelly place.

Even though he'd been assured Wentworth was again at his estate near Kent, he had no desire to view the ship he'd captained and Jonathan had served on years ago. All the gold and blue did nothing but remind him of his viscount, which sank him deeper into melancholy.

Yet here he was, because Jonathan was exceptionally persuasive.

"This outing will get you out of the doldrums. Give us back my happy Hector." Jonathan jumped down from the carriage and held the door open.

A curse of frustration lodged in the back of his throat. He was wholly sick of being treated like a toy.

Squinting into the glaring midmorning sun, he stepped out of the carriage and looked up at an enormous sailing vessel. He counted three masts and three rows of gun ports. The lettering on her aft read *Neptune*.

"Fought with Lord Nelson at Trafalgar," said Jonathan. "In port for repairs. God only knows why it's taken so long to get her shipshape again."

They walked down the pier, Jonathan driving him past other vessels with his hand on Hector's lower back. He wanted to brush off the steering touch, but more importantly, he did not want a public confrontation. Not that anyone would notice with hundreds of dockworkers and military men rushing about and shouting orders.

He took a deep breath despite the stink, put his shoulders back, and vowed to get this over with. Afterward he'd leave Jonathan and start the beginning of the rest of his life.

He had additional ideas for his porcelain factory and was looking forward to having more time to implement his concepts. He'd managed to keep Jonathan in the dark about his purchase, wanting to keep that part of his life selfishly to himself. But now he needed to focus on what direction to take the factory to continue their gain in profits and keep the workers safe and productive.

He was so engrossed with his business designs, he almost missed Jonathan's nudge to a gangboard leading to the rear end of a warship with three masts and two rows of guns.

"Here she is," said Jonathan. "The *Dragon*. The most fearless vessel to ever sail the seven seas."

It was smaller than the *Neptune* but no less impressive. Hector climbed up the gangboard, wishing for something he could cling to—a railing, a rope, a strong supportive hand.

❖

"Look up there." Jon pointed at a small yellow flag. "That means the captain is not on board." The lying came so easily to him. "The white one lets the sailors know which way the wind blows."

"Really?" Hector stopped and gazed at the tapered pendant, his odd brows pinching together against the sun's glare. "I would think it ill-advisable to announce to any and all ne'er-do-wells that the captain is on shore, looking for a whore."

Laughing, Jon said, "Ah, but everyone knows what superb first mates the British Admiralty puts in charge when the captains are on shore leave." He winked at Hector, who wore a jacket that had grown too large for him over the past months. Making an effort, he squeezed one thin shoulder.

Just a bit more patience. After today, his life would be clear and pleasing forever. He touched Hector's thin, firm back again and whispered so only he could hear, "Let us go, love. I have something I very much want to show you."

Chapter Sixteen

Wentworth returned to his ship to evade maudlin thoughts, but the beauty of hundreds of men—men with balance, grace, some with swaying braids, bared chests and tanned skin, others in officers' finely tailored blues—only reminded him of what he had lost. His beautiful boy. He should not have come here today.

The HBMS *Dragon* was docked for small repairs and refitting as needed. When everything was shipshape, she would serve as a training vessel and patrol the channel until something exciting happened with the French. He hoped that was sooner rather than later. A good battle would put his mood back to rights.

Until then, he had a competent crew who could see to everything. There was no need to be here. He was there nonetheless, waiting for his three midshipmen to return with news.

The creak of wood and the sway underfoot gave him a sense of being home, but the rough timbre of William's warm tenor behind him no longer elicited the same effect.

At one time Wentworth would have given one hundred pounds just to hear William's voice in the captain's cabin. He looked out the open window to the Thames, choppy in the receding tide.

"Ty, did you hear me?" Will had carried on a bland dissertation on the merits of doubling the number of backstays for the mast. Normally the conversation would have entertained him and he would have started a rigorous debate. Normally. Not today.

Today that voice was just a little deeper and a little rougher than the one he longed to hear. Since the cadence and word choice was similar to Hector's, Wentworth could imagine him standing in his cabin instead of Will, lying in his bed naked, arms and legs open, inviting.

He swallowed the lump rising from the depths of his gut. "I…" He cleared his throat. "I agree. Some extra ropes could be advantageous."

"What? You agree?"

"Of course."

"You never agree."

"Will, I find myself asking you the same question every time I see you. But at the risk of being redundant, I must ask again. Why are you here?"

No response. He looked over his shoulder. Head bent, Will ran a hand through his chronically disheveled hair. It did not lie in naturally neat, alluring curls like Hector's. "Will?"

"Actually, I went to your town house first."

"William!"

"Mary said I should come."

"You came because Mary said so?"

"Well, truth be told, she convinced me you could help us set Hector back to rights."

"How insightful of her. As it turns out, I agree."

Will looked at his shoes. "Mary is a very perceptive person, Ty. She also convinced me that I missed your friendship." Will snorted, shot out of his chair, and paced to the door, his limp marring what used to be the flawless, graceful stride Hector shared.

"I see. Your wife is an amazing woman, Will. Suggesting we rekindle our friendship after what I did to her—what you and I did…together."

Will shoved his fists into his coat pockets and slowly turned around. "I'm not certain 'rekindle' is what she has in mind, but she cares about her family, and for some reason, she thinks *I believe* you should still be part of the fold." He laughed, but it sounded more sad than humorous. "As many times as you protected us from Father, I felt sometimes I should have given you a chance to explain. She must have surmised I miss the friendship we once had when I mentioned the thrashing we received after the rabbit, Indian headdress, and gooseberry pie incident."

"Bloody hell, Will. That was the most humiliating day of my life. I never tell anyone else about that. Well, perhaps I did once. But I will point out the fact that your participation did not sit well with the adults either. I'm surprised you shared that tale with your wife. God, to this day I still hate gooseberries."

"Well, I might have left out some of the facts. So, are you willing to work with me to help Hector out of the doldrums?"

His stomach felt very peculiar. He had the chance to get back what he had thought was the most important relationship in his life, and it was offered so casually, as if it were no more important than what to have for supper.

"Damn it, Ty, do you have to make this difficult for me?"

Despite his glum mood, he felt a surge of smug satisfaction. He'd suffered more than two years of hell when Will cut him out of his life, so he planned to enjoy this. He fought to keep the twitching corners of his mouth from turning up. He was only marginally successful. "Must admit there is a certain gratification in the event, but I will take you back without making you grovel."

Will's face went from contrite to pinched in the time it would have taken a cannonball to clear the main deck, so Wentworth decided to end his friend's misery. "There was a time when you recognized my humor."

"Damn it." Will plunged his hand through his hair again. "This *is* difficult for me. You're right. I need to take my ease."

"I agree with you there."

Will's shoulders stiffened.

Wentworth held out a hand to stop the brewing firestorm. "I gave you good reason to end the friendship. Believe me, I have regretted my actions every day since then." He walked over to Will. "Friends?"

Will shook Wentworth's proffered hand longer and more vigorously than needed. The hand was firm, calloused, with a broad palm and fingers. Not strong and elegant like Hector's. "I will let you ask me again when this is all over, and we shall decide then."

"Understood." He added, "I did not know. That Greig was insane. I did not know."

Will's sad smile was crooked, the scar across his cheek pulling the skin just so.

Unlike his brother, Will was not radiant and full of excitement to see the world and experience new things. His touch no longer elicited a surge of arousal, no longer provoked a need to possess.

Wentworth had failed with Hector, but he planned to make it up to him, to try and make Hector his once more even though he knew he did not deserve this pure, sweet soul with appalling taste in men.

Figuring out how to win him back was the difficult part.

Getting Jonathan away from him was the easy role in this duplicity.

"Now, back to the topic that brought you here. As I mentioned, I was a prick to Hector. However, I do not think that is why he is beaten down." He turned and looked at Will, who stood, feet apart, head tilted to the right just enough that Wentworth knew his full, potent attention was on the problem. "I received a letter from Jonathan that disturbed me. He sounded…well, not fully in control. I went to see Hector after you left yesterday."

"Of all the—"

"Just listen, Will. You should realize by now I seldom do what people command of me."

Will pursed his lips but remained quiet.

"Lieutenant Jonathan Baker was at Hector's rooms. The visit did not go well. In fact, Hector told me to leave."

"And you did?"

"Yes. I saw no good coming of my staying. Yesterday an anonymous letter waited for me, but I know it was from Jonathan. He gloated about his conquest of Hector. Talked about the *things* he'd done to him. Described the things he would do soon. He detailed things that no sane person could tolerate—pain, desecration, demoralizations." Bloody damn hell! His insides cramped, and he thought he might cry for the first time in decades. "I think most of the letter was lies, but…"

Will clenched his fists. "Why would he send you a letter about his involvement with Hector?"

"You will not like the answer to that question. God knows I have fretted over it since receiving the missive."

"Just tell me."

"Jonathan and I had an on-and-off affair. He was more

interested than I. Since I found him convenient, I kept the door open to him."

"I expected as much." Will sighed. "You are intent on self-destruction, aren't you? That man is meaner than a caged tiger."

"Yes, well, that was part of the draw, I suppose."

"Bloody hell, Ty."

"Will, my past is immaterial right now. What is important is Hector's health. As I said, I came to London to set the matter straight, and I know how to do that." Taking a deep breath, he ignored the feeling of inadequacy. "If I confront Jonathan, he will dig in his heels because he knows he is disturbing me. Why that gives him pleasure I do not know. The man is quite confounding. And since I imagine Hector still will not talk to me at this point, I must take action."

Will paced. "I will talk with Hector and demand he stop seeing that shit for an excuse of a navy officer."

"That is about as likely to work as if I talk with Jonathan. No, something more forceful is needed, and I set things in motion. Trust me on this and drop the matter for now."

"Zero chance of that happening, Ty. Might as well tell me, or I'll be your shadow for the next week. You won't be able to piss without wetting my shoes."

Wentworth sighed, knowing Will's loyalty to his family would ensure he kept that threat. "If I tell you, do not try to convince me this is a bad idea. Do not try to involve yourself, and do not get upset because it reminds you of something I did in the past."

Will laughed, an irony-filled sound. "What, you talked some officers into serving him fake papers to get him on a ship immediately and out of the country as soon as the tide rises, so you can work on Hector?"

Wentworth's blood ran cold. He stood very still, waiting for the cannon explosion.

"Bloody hell, Ty. You never learn."

"It works. Why struggle to invent a new technique that has yet to be tested?"

"You cannot twiddle with people's lives as if you are omniscient and know what is best for everyone. You—"

"Will, be quiet."

"I will not."

"Please, just listen." He walked back to the window, needing a lungful of outside air suddenly. The cabin seemed exceedingly constricting. "I sent three of my largest, cruelest crew members dressed as officers, just in case Jonathan does not believe the ruse, but you surmised the rest of my plan. They are waiting until Jonathan leaves Hector's rooms.

"I must get him away from Hector, and I know this tactic will work. The man is bad to the marrow and will do nothing but harm your brother. Once he is out of the country, I will apologize to Hector, tell him how important he is to me. He likely will not listen, but he will think Jonathan left him to go on a lark. Even if he does not want me ever again, it will be a sure bet he will not accept Jonathan again either, since it will appear he slipped off without telling Hector he was leaving. And if Jonathan does return and starts sniffing around Hector again, I'll have him tied and thrown into the bilge water."

"When will you carry this plan out?"

"My men are already watching and waiting for him. Hopefully he will leave Hector's house alone soon, in time to get him onto the *Ariadne* before she sails for a three-month patrol duty. If not, they will call at Hector's rooms tonight and give him his new orders. Granted, that will not be as effective, but if, during Jonathan's absence, you can offhandedly tell

Hector about a man you know called Red Jon who has been acting foolish around whorehouses and molly houses, that will cement an aversion in Hector's mind. He will agree to never see Jonathan again. It will work. Trust me on this matter."

Wentworth turned at Will's silence.

"As much as I hate to admit my thoughts, it does seem like a sound strategy. Is there anything else I can do? I feel so useless right now."

"Well then, look over the documents I forged for Jonathan's captain. Let me know if you see anything that will alert the admiralty to the duplicity."

They modified the documents and discussed the plan. After deciding they would bid Mary to join in their little deception—surely she would agree to cheer Hector after his second disastrous relationship in one year—he clasped Will's shoulder. "Come, let me show you the improvements I've made to the *Dragon* since you turned into a landlubber."

Hand on Will's broad back, he ushered him out of the captain's quarters to the sun-drenched quarterdeck. He would win Hector back. He didn't want anyone else, and he couldn't countenance seeing Hector with anyone else. They were meant to be together, he now knew, and he would make it happen.

With a freedom of spirit he'd not felt in years, he followed Will up smoothly worn steps, not even tempted to ogle his arse.

Chapter Seventeen

Jonathan led Hector to the rear of the ship, pointing out things like the main mast and quarterdeck. He stood on a highly polished deck near the rear of the ship, on the side facing the deepest portion of the Thames. the sun warmed his face as a breeze caressed the back of Hector's head. *Strange...Doesn't the breeze blow inland from the water?*

"Stand right there." Jonathan leaned in and whispered with unusually moist breath, "You are exceptionally fine-looking today."

Hector suppressed the urge to wipe his face. Other than the spittle, he was surprised. Just like that, Jonathan had given him a compliment. A *real* compliment. No *but*, no *if*, nothing other than comforting words meant to uplift. If only this had started weeks ago...months ago.

He'd almost forgotten how good a compliment could feel. He smiled his first smile in what felt like years.

Watching the near-perfect form of Jonathan walk away, Hector enjoyed his masculine beauty. Too bad beauty wasn't enough.

Hector didn't love Jonathan. Really, didn't even respect him. Perhaps if he knew more about the lieutenant's military accomplishments. Maybe he'd saved countless lives during battle or saved the vessel from colliding with rocks on a foggy night. But he didn't know any of these things. Jonathan had only told of how many Frogs and French allies he'd killed. It was hard to love, even like, someone who put such value on violence.

Never having been on a boat before, he was rather surprised at the clutter and frenzied activity. Sailors ran this way carrying ropes and that way carrying piles of cloth. Looking up at the top of the masts gave him a sense of vertigo that made him want to laugh like a child on his birthday. He wouldn't mind spending a few days at sea. It must be amazing to be on the ocean with the wind brushing your face and propelling you to a distant land.

He wanted to explore the deck but decided to wait by the railing and see whatever Jonathan was so immensely proud of. Tomorrow he would gently break off the relationship. A clean break. Better that way. Like removing a splinter.

In public would be best, given Jonathan's temper. *What exactly to say?* He'd figure that out tonight, probably in the wee hours of the morning, since he couldn't get any rest with this task weighing on his mind.

Why couldn't Jonathan have been as beautiful on the inside as on the outside? Then he could have settled down with him and been content, if not completely happy. He would always miss Wentworth, even if he found someone else to love. Wentworth possessed everything he had ever wanted in a man and in a lover. He was the only man Hector had ever fallen in love with, but the arse could not be trusted.

Jonathan was scurrying along a wide, horizontal pole, and Hector, unable to look at him while unfaithful thoughts ran through his mind, looked away and saw something that made the world seem to drop from beneath his feet.

A few seconds later, half-recovered from the shock, he

felt the wooden planking keeping him aloft, but he could no longer feel himself breathe. He gulped in air.

Twenty feet away on the quarterdeck stood the captain, staring right at him. Wentworth's fists clenched, knuckles white with strain, lips moving to form Hector's name.

Remembering all the pain Wentworth caused him, he renewed his resolve to stand firm, to not swallow his pride and try again to capture and keep this beast's heart. His smile faltered, and he started to turn away from the railing.

He only had a brief moment to notice Wentworth's features falling into a mask of pure horror as he yelled, "No!"

What the—

A beam struck Hector in the chest. Air rushed out of his lungs in an excruciating gush. His lower back hit the railing, and then there was nothing below or above him but air before he plunged into the muddy Thames.

CHAPTER EIGHTEEN

Angels above, Hector was handsome, Wentworth thought. The harsh sun picked out the red-brown in his dark hair. He was not just handsome, he was perfect—exactly like Wentworth remembered him the past lonely months. Ever since awakening from his fog about the events that happened almost two years ago, he realized how completely desirable Hector was in his own right, not at all a pale substitute for William.

Hector stood on the gun deck of his *Dragon*, his hair rumpled from the wind. He'd lost weight, but he still looked tall and strong and perfect.

He is here. He came. Why? Did he come to find me, to talk to me? Did he come to say he was free and wanted to try again? Hector did not look overly happy, however. His dark brows, drawn together, gave him a pensive air.

Wentworth prayed to a god he'd ignored for twenty years. *Let him be free. Let him be here for me.*

At that moment, Hector noticed him and smiled...no, he *radiated* happiness. Wentworth's heart swelled to near bursting and beat out a call to arms. He smiled back, not even caring if rekindling his relationship with Hector would ruin his new, tentative friendship with Will.

Three men in officers' uniforms clambered onto the

Dragon. Why the hell were his henchmen back? They should have been shadowing Jonathan.

Wentworth heard a chopping sound, followed by a creak and a groan that should not occur on a docked ship. The stern boom, its sail unfurled, snapped toward starboard. He did not even have to look; he knew instinctively where it would swing. He yelled, but deep inside, he knew it was too late. He bounded up the stairs to the quarterdeck, his feet still on the stairs as Hector's body tumbled overboard.

He'd seen this happen twice before, and both seamen had died. The same would not happen to Hector. He would not let it. His feet hit the deck, and in two bounds, he dived over the side into the deadly black Thames.

CHAPTER NINETEEN

Will saw Jonathan sneering by the foremast, but it took him critical seconds to understand what he saw. He let his dagger fly, but he reacted two seconds too late.

Mayhem ensued.

Will turned at Ty's yell just in time to see Hector tossed overboard. What the hell was he doing here anyway? Ty, defying gravity while kicking off shoes, flew to the point where Hector had tipped into the river, struggling out of his jacket. Then he dived overboard. Four other seamen heeded his command to follow and dived in right behind him.

Some or all of them would need help getting out of the water, especially with the retreating tide. Will began barking orders as if he were still a naval man. Men grabbed hooks to drape over the side, but the tide carried everyone out of reach too fast to be hooked from on deck.

Dinghies dropped from their ropes into the water only moments after Will's order. Time being critical, they couldn't afford to slowly lower the first few, so he hoped at least some would land topside up. He scrambled down a ladder, more slide and fall than ordered descent.

Good God. They had to live. Hector, his beloved little brother, and Ty, the man who as a boy protected him and Hector from a drunken father. They both had to live.

He jumped into the closest dinghy.

He would not let them die.

Taking up oars, he scanned the surface for heads, cloth, air bubbles, bodies.

God, they could not die!

❖

Hector's bones ached from the cold.

He felt cold but snuggled into blankets so fine, they conformed to every inch of his skin. Hector blinked. It was so dark and cold and somehow strangely comfortable. He closed his eyes, enjoying the lack of pain. He'd been in pain recently, desperate, consuming pain from a hurt that lived in his heart, not his body. So he embraced the cold numbness, treasured it, reached for and welcomed oblivion.

Slowly, a burning in his lungs grew bonfire hot. The burning was relentless. He reached for the sensation, but his fingers tangled in wet cloth. He was underwater. *What the...?*

Instinctual need expanded his lungs, but the flood of water set him to coughing, and he inhaled more water. His only hope was to make the surface. He kicked and pushed toward the light glowing overhead as his body jerked and spasmed, fighting for air.

But the light only grew dimmer. He sank and sank to a lonely, cold depth away from any warmth.

Away from any hope of love.

Away from Wentworth.

❖

Wentworth could see nothing. *Damnation, damn it all!*

The bloody Thames was too murky this time of year to see

anything, and his damnably wet clothes kept dragging at him, slowing him down. He desperately ripped at his shirt. The fight to free himself from his clothes kept him from concentrating on swimming. He sank farther, drawn down by cold, unforgiving water. He did not fight to surface for breath. He had to be able to swim unhampered or he would never find Hector, so he kept ripping and pulling until the clinging cloth surged away with the tide. He kicked to the surface and scanned the area even while he pulled air into his starved lungs.

A handful of his sailors bobbed up and down on the waves. A few buoys bounced across the surface in different directions. No Hector.

Fear sawed at his gut, and he almost doubled over from the instant pain. Hector could not be dead. With renewed desperation, Wentworth dived under, using all his senses to detect movement, warmth, anything. This got him no closer to finding the man he loved.

He had to consider the current. Kicking to the surface, he judged where Hector fell in and approximated by the tug on his legs how far the current would have pulled an unconscious, fully clothed body. He swam with the current and renewed his search.

❖

Will's voice cracked from issuing order after order across noisy waves. He'd sent the dinghies downriver, knowing Hector would be pulled along at several knots with the receding tide.

Four sailors' heads bobbed to the surface for air, and then each dived again, all of them looking for Will's little brother.

They had about as much chance of finding a diamond in a coal mine.

The last time Will had seen Hector, they had argued. Will

had dug for reasons, but Hector refused to tell him anything. Will had let his temper get the better of him, and he realized they both needed time to cool off before addressing the topic again, so Will eventually stormed away.

Now he might never have the chance to apologize.

He scrubbed the blur from his eyes and finally located Ty, who was swimming downriver like a man possessed.

Will ordered the men in his boat to redirect and follow.

Chapter Twenty

With renewed strength, Hector drove his legs. Now they burned as badly as his water-filled lungs. His whole body burned from lack of air, but he would not give up until all his muscles failed. He would not leave this earth until he found out what that last smile on Wentworth's face had promised.

The dinghy's sallow brown light came slowly closer. He pulled toward it with arms that felt like logs.

Hours seemed to pass before his head breached the surface. He gasped in air and coughed it out. Panic set in, and he lost conscious control over his arms and legs, managing to grab one half-breath before sinking beneath the surface. His limbs lost strength; his starved lungs were still waterlogged. He coughed and breathed in the thick, muddy water.

Trashing about from the raw pain of wet lungs, his body refused the command to swim. He took another, then another breath of water. His muscles calmed. He felt the cold.

He sank.

❖

Wentworth rapidly lost hope. Even with his expert understanding of currents, it was next to impossible to determine where to look for Hector. His chest hurt. Was this what it felt like to have a heart seizure?

Swiveling around, he looked for anything to hint at Hector's location. A ripple that went against the river waves, bubbles, anything.

Finally, about ten yards away, a bedraggled head surfaced—Hector gasping, choking, flailing. The stringy wet-haired head was the most beautiful thing he had ever seen. He swam as fast as a porpoise, the current giving him speed, but the boy slipped under. He dived, the muddy witch's brew churning with the current change, making it impossible to see.

Long ago, Wentworth stopped believing in God, but just then there must have been a divine intervention, for he felt a subtle warmth to his right. He grasped in desperation and clutched on to cloth.

Heart about to burst from exertion, he gathered his remaining strength and pulled the limp form close. He clung to it with desperation, clutching at Hector's cold body. Fear gripped him, giving him a last bit of strength to surface, but he squeezed Hector harder than intended, causing the boy to spasm.

He would hold on to his love forever, never letting go. If he never let go, then Hector could not die.

Or they would die together.

❖

Strong, warm arms held him. Such a pleasant feeling… floating…sheltered. Hector smiled, or at least he thought he smiled.

But then the arms squeezed too hard, and acid hot water rushed from his lungs and he coughed and then dragged in air that felt like fire. Choking, fighting the pain, he almost went under again, but those strong arms held his mouth mere inches above the surface, keeping him from breathing in more water.

People yelled all around. He tried to open his eyes, but all he could do was cough and spit up water. Something tried to pull him away from his warm, safe refuge. He fought, tried to scream *stop*, but all he could do was cough. With lots of pulling, ripping, and angling, he lost the strong arms from around his waist and was lifted out of the water.

He tried to complain, but instead he choked on waterless air before vomiting on someone's shoe.

❖

"Ty! Let him go," Will yelled, his voice rough.

Wentworth held on to the struggling form in his arms. He would not let go and take the chance that Hector would slip back under the cold, dark water.

Then arms like steel grasped him, and someone else pulled Hector away. They stole his young lover. Wentworth clung to Hector's trouser leg with all his strength and shouted like a wild beast scaring away death.

"Ty, you idiot. Get in the dinghy before you both drown," yelled William. "Ty! I have him. I will keep him safe."

He almost did not let go, but some thread of rational thought surfaced, and he allowed them to pull Hector the rest of the way into the tiny rocking craft.

When all sound died save waves against wood, he bellowed and grabbed for anything he could reach to pull himself out of the river. Others pulled, and he was unceremoniously dumped into the dinghy, his nose an inch away from sloshing water.

He pushed up, looking for Hector. He lay over Will's legs, his white fingers balled into fists as Will worked to clear all the water from Hector's lungs and stomach.

On shaking arms and legs, Wentworth half crawled, half climbed over planks so he could pull him back into his arms, when he heard the most welcome sound in the world, the sound of Hector gasping in a breath.

"Hooray," he yelled as Hector, who was beautifully, amazingly alive, hacked up Thames water all over Will's shoe. He was so pale and vulnerable, limp in the belly of the craft, his head resting on Will's arm, his chest slumped across Will's legs, panting.

Wentworth knelt by Hector and rubbed his cold, wet form. When Hector was able to sit up, Wentworth shoved Will away and worked off Hector's sodden cravat, hoping that would help the boy get air.

Hector turned and blinked at him with big brown eyes, lashes clumped together with moisture. He said nothing, just looked and blinked. Damp hair clung to his skull and cheeks.

Wentworth unbuttoned Hector's ruined coat and shirt, stripping them off as someone dropped a dry topcoat over the half-drowned man.

He found a rapidly growing bruise and a stretch of scraped, bleeding skin. He touched Hector's ribs, and the boy flinched. "You're injured," he said, feeling less than brilliant. "Where else are you hurt?"

Hector opened his mouth, but instead of words all that came out were racking coughs. He shook his head instead.

"Do not speak. We will get you to the ship, and Will can attend to you. He shall make you well. We won't let you die." Wentworth barely registered how stupid he sounded or the thickness clogging his words. "God. I thought you were gone. Gone before I could convince you I love you."

Hector stopped blinking and stared with those big, wide eyes.

Wentworth pulled him close and kissed warmth into his

icy lips. He took a deep breath and registered Hector's smell, and a slow, deep contentment settled into his bones.

He pulled away slowly, and for a brief, wonderful moment their lips stuck as if they too never wanted to part. Hector's eyes slid closed.

A soft, whistled version of "Paddy, Lay Back" captured his attention. *What the hell!*

He turned. Four of his men shared the boat with them, all looking off in different directions. Midshipman Smitty pursed his lips and continued the bawdy melody.

Will stared right at them, his jaw muscles working. Looking murderous.

What the bloody hell had he been thinking, jeopardizing not only himself but Hector as well. His self-chastisement was not as scathing as the scornful black glare from Hector's brother.

To save face, he said loud enough for all to hear over the slap of water on the side of the boat, "I am just glad he is not dead, is all. And if a kiss was in order for Admiral Nelson, then…"

Hector croaked. "I've had enough water to last me several seasons. Would someone take me to shore?"

CHAPTER TWENTY-ONE

Will's dagger buried deep in his chest, Jonathan had trouble breathing. Before, it had only hurt like hell, but now it was worse than pain. It was like dragging a twenty-one gunner through a canal with a two-ply rope around his torso.

"Open your eyes."

Wentworth's cherished deep voice pulled him away from his suffering. He obeyed as Wentworth leaned over him, dripping water onto the deck.

Jonathan pushed back a lock of Wentworth's wet, black hair with his trembling hand and pulled in another breath. They were harder and harder to take. "Dear one..." The words bubbled out, moist and blood thick. "We can be together now. You are mine. Only mine. Hector can no longer come between us."

Wentworth took hold of Jonathan's hand and rested it on Jonathan's struggling chest. With a sad smile, Wentworth said, "Yes, well, we can talk about that after you get some sleep."

Another breath. "Together?"

A pause. "Of course. Now rest. You must be tired."

Joy filled his heart. "Yes, very tired, mine own." He closed his eyes.

❖

Crouched on the deck near a pool of blood, Wentworth watched Jonathan choke on his last breath.

Such a waste. At one time, Jonathan had been a fine sailor, a confidant, but through the years, something changed. Had jealousy eaten away his sanity? Had some tropical disease altered his perception of right and wrong to the point where he was capable of murder?

He looked at the dagger in Jonathan's chest. Blood covered his once pristine navy coat and strong hands, dried in his beautiful red-blond hair.

Such a damnable waste.

He yanked the ebony-and-pearl-handled dagger from the dead man's chest and slipped it into his waistband.

He called to the nearest man, unable to see who it was through teary eyes. "Clean him up and prepare him for services. Tomorrow Lieutenant Thompson will take him to sea. Make certain the chaplain is aboard by morning." He turned toward his cabin for a shirt and coat and then left his *Dragon*, not even bothering to rub his hands free of blood.

Chapter Twenty-Two

Hector pulled the blanket tighter with one hand and held a hot toddy in the other. The piping-hot bath had stopped the chills, but he still felt gravestone cold. Jonathan had tried to kill him. The frigid Thames water was nothing compared to that realization.

He sipped the steaming, bittersweet liquid and watched Will pace, but tried to ignore his ranting.

"I cannot believe he did that in plain view of probably one hundred men." Will crossed to the burgundy wall of his town house guest room, turned on his heel, then went back to the other wall. "Kissing you. God!"

Hector closed his eyes. The memory of Wentworth's lips on his warmed him better than the blanket and the toddy.

Turn. Pace. "Of all the ill-conceived notions that man has come up with over the years, that is without doubt the most idiotic and dangerous." Turn. Pace.

He stopped. "And then making that damning declaration, saying he loves you, within mere feet from four of his men."

Hector almost dropped the whisky-laced coffee. "What did you say?"

Will didn't answer, just continued to pace and grouse.

Love? Hector had convinced himself that his imagination

and the dreadful cold had conjured up that declaration. Suddenly he felt warmed throughout. Almost hot, in fact.

Wentworth loved him? When had that happened? He shook his head but smiled. He couldn't help it. The muscles of his face took over, and with the stretch of lips came a lifting of his spirits. He drained the cup.

"I cannot believe the risk he took. Put you both in danger, he did. Good thing his crew will do anything for him. Damnedest thing. They treat him like a revered father, even though he is younger than many of them."

Standing up, Hector winced at the pain. Even with his chest wrapped tightly, Will said he would be in pain for months. Since his ribs did not seem broken, just badly bruised, he ignored the ache. He had things to do, so he would not sit about like an invalid.

He was strong and capable and in control of his life, just like his two older brothers. He could do anything he set his mind to. And right now, he had a mind to kiss one very difficult viscount.

"Good thing he will have to go to headquarters and deal with reporting what that murdering bastard Jonathan tried to pull today. Never did trust that man. If Wentworth were here, I would have a month-old ration of shit to give him. I want you to stay away from him, Hector. He almost got you killed today because of his relationship with Jonathan, and then to…" Will threw his hands up in the air.

Hector smiled like a simpleton. "No. No, actually, I have a feeling I will see quite a lot of Wentworth from here on out." He turned away from Will's gaping expression and went to the wardrobe to find clothes. Fortunately, Mary had seen fit to send a servant around to his rooms to collect things he would need.

He suspected he would see Wentworth very soon, in fact,

and he needed to look his best for the questioning he planned to give him. He was infuriating but desirable as hell, even when dripping wet and stinking of the Thames.

He dressed, slowly and painfully, while Will continued his tirade.

Hector still wanted commitment. But even if Wentworth would not give him that, he might still have an affair with the man. *After all*—he smiled to himself—*he does claim to love me.*

He left the room.

"Hector, have you heard anything I've just said? Hector? Damn it, Heckie."

CHAPTER TWENTY-THREE

"His record lists increasing signs of destructive behavior over the past five years. Seems it was only a matter of time before he did something to hurt himself or someone else," Admiral Chambers said.

Wentworth listened and ground his teeth. Knowing Jonathan had grown increasingly unstable should have relieved some of the remorse twisting his gut. It did not.

"Did you know he was on forced leave this past year?"

Wentworth shook his head.

"Captain Hodges reported Lieutenant Baker was not to return to duty until he could treat his fellow officers with respect and decency. No specifics noted, however."

"When we were midshipmen together, he was a fine officer candidate."

"Not everyone improves with age as you and I have." Admiral Chambers chuckled, the sound like glass shards on Wentworth's frayed sentiments. "As I see it, your report is sufficient. No need for a formal investigation. You are free to go. Will you remain on the *Dragon* to ensure your men are calm and orderly after this event?"

No! It would be days, if not weeks, before he could stomach climbing aboard his beloved girl again. "No, the crew is in good hands, and I need to wash and change before seeing to an errand. Then I will check on the health of young Somerville. I imagine Dr. Somerville will have me strung up if his little brother does not recover from his mishap on the *Dragon*."

That glass-grating chuckle again. Wentworth would not make it through this interview without demotion unless he left soon.

"That Dr. Somerville does have a soft spot for family, does he not? We lost a good officer when he married and left the navy."

Wentworth smiled for the benefit of his superior. "Yes, but he can be downright annoying at times." He turned to leave, thinking Will's soft spot for family just might allow Hector the freedom to love whom he wished and still be accepted into the fold.

"And do make good on your wish to get clean before you go anywhere else, Captain. Bathe away that unsightly blood. It's not the image the Admiralty wants to portray."

He looked down. There was lots of blood, dried and browning. Ignoring the painful memories of watching a man die, he rubbed Jonathan's life force off his hands, onto his coat.

Just like that, evidence of a once-vibrant man could be wiped away.

CHAPTER TWENTY-FOUR

Stepping into Will's house after all these years, all these events, all the hatred, would have been impossible, but he had to see Hector and ensure he was indeed well. The foyer looked the same, but the place felt larger, more intimidating.

"You!" Just one word, spat out as if rancid.

He turned slowly but ducked before Will's blow could land true, taking a clip on his ear instead of a facer.

Will readied to deliver the next, but Wentworth yelled, "Stop!" and held up the blood-crusted dagger.

Will sneered at him. "He set the scene. Purposely tried to kill Hector because of your liaison with both of them. You toy with people. You toyed with them. Boys. Men. And then you made a public declaration of love to my—"

"I am no saint, Will, but are my actions worse than yours? You killed a man today. You killed Lieutenant Jonathan Baker, after he acted. Who of us is the least moral man standing here?"

Will snatched his dagger. "I acted in the heat of battle, trying to save lives. I did not know what other dangers the man intended."

"And I acted out of love. I think you know that emotion. You would behave the same way if Mary were raised from a watery grave alive."

Will had always been a fair man, ruthless in battle and quick to judge but fair when the situation lay in front of him. He nodded, turned, and looked up the stairwell.

Hector stood fifteen feet above them. The energetic boy was strangely still, but beautiful, *alive*, vibrant despite the total lack of motion.

Suddenly the house was as it should be, warm and inviting. Cozy.

Hector's wet hair was slicked back and clean. He almost glowed with vitality, better than the last few times Wentworth had seen him. Hell, better than he had ever seen him. The skin around his mouth lay smooth, not pinched, and the hollows under his eyes were gone. A slight, hesitant smile—beautiful. *Alive*, for God's sake. Alive.

Wentworth took a step forward. His heart filled with a painful swell of hope before his stomach knotted and he realized what the sad smile must mean. This was it. The end.

Even though it would almost kill him, he hoped Hector would make good decisions from now on. Find someone worthy of his love who would love him back, without baggage and conditions. Someone who would realize they loved him before losing him. Someone who would freely offer him forever.

"Are you well?"

"Well enough." His voice was rough and raspy.

"You were so strong, so brave." Wentworth swallowed the lump thickening his voice. "I have never seen anyone else survive a similar fate. You saved yourself."

"I did, didn't I?" Hector's smile grew almost to his typical gaiety. "With a little help, it seems." He walked slowly but seductively down the stairs. The seductive part came naturally for him. The imp could not help his sensual nature.

Wentworth decided to open the cauldron and let every-thing out. He was tired of the constant fight within his head. "I thought I lost you before I could tell you I love you."

Hector stopped on the last step.

Rubbing a hand over his aching chest, Wentworth licked his lips. "I want to be honest with you. Hell, I need to be honest with myself too. I have always wanted to be normal. I never truly believed two men"—he looked around; Will had left them alone—"could have what you reached for. Your devotion, freely given, was quite petrifying."

"Love in any form cannot be wrong," Hector whispered. "You and I just love differently than some."

"I have learned the truth of that, Hector. When you and I were first together, you were so accepting of our liaison, so engaging and beautiful, it was no time at all before I was in love. But I fought the emotion. I never wanted to be hurt again, and you were so much like your brother, who hurt me to the quick. I was afraid history would repeat itself. Every time you reminded me of Will, I was reminded of the rejection and the pain it caused." He laughed at his pathetic history and illogical emotions. "It makes no sense, I know. I suppose emotions and desires do not make sense most of the time. My fear, on top of, well, guilt, was unbearable. I wanted to forget. Most of the time I did forget, but in so doing, I also forgot what you meant to me. I had loved you beyond anything once. Finally, I remember."

"And now?"

A slow, warm fire built in his belly. Why had it taken him so long to be able to admit how he felt? What an asinine idiot he had been all his life. "Now I again love you beyond anything." He shook his head. "So much time wasted."

"Well, I am afraid we will waste more time, since I need

convincing you truly know what you want. Come, I will order tea and you will pour." Hector strolled past very close, his shirt sleeve almost rubbing Wentworth's chest as he walked down the corridor and left Wentworth standing in the entryway.

CHAPTER TWENTY-FIVE

Early summer 1809, London

Will chuckled to himself and watched Mary put little Margaret down for the night. "Come down to the drawing room when you're done there, my love."

She looked up with those large, light brown eyes he loved so dearly, a small contented smile brightening her heart-shaped face.

Earlier that week he'd smuggled in a bottle of her favorite tawny port and planned to put it to good use. They'd been too busy of late, dealing with their toddler, setting up a laboratory for Mary's mathematical studies, and watching Hector closely to make certain he fully recovered from his ordeals. He was past the dangerous stage of near drowning, and he never developed a fever or a worsening cough.

Now that Hector was safe, he felt the need to celebrate his happiness with Mary. As soon as she came downstairs for afternoon tea, he planned to seduce her. The port was an added measure to help her relax. Several days had passed since they'd made love, and he planned to end their dry spell within the hour.

Opening the door to the drawing room proved challenging

with port, stemware, blanket, and the wrapped silver necklace he had purchased on a whim a few days ago. The glasses clinked when he reached for the slipping blanket and stepped inside.

"Damnation," Wentworth said as Hector laughed. "Forgot to lock the door." They were lying on the carpet near the hearth, both bare to the waist. Hector's trousers were loose, as though they'd been pulled shut in a hurry.

"Ty," Will said, surprised. "I thought you two left an hour ago. What the hell are you still…? Are you fucking?"

"No. Not fucking yet, Will, but soon. Very, very soon."

Hector's chuckle was almost a snort, of all things. The little bugger at least had the decency to duck his head behind Ty's shoulder. But Ty, just as bold as a sultan in his harem, smiled up at Will, showing his white teeth.

"Damn it, Ty, when will you stop putting Hector at risk of discovery? What are you thinking?"

"I admit to not thinking today, just feeling."

"You should be ashamed of your recklessness. Both of you."

Ty touched his forehead to Hector's. "No. I am not ashamed. I am in love."

Hector opened his mouth as if to say something, but nothing came out.

"But the danger?" Will said.

Ty turned to look at him, stroking Hector's cheek with one hand. "I will be careful, of that you can be assured, but I am not ashamed, Will." He leaned down and kissed Hector, as bold as you please.

"Good God. Not in my house. Take it somewhere else if you can't keep your hands off each other." But he realized he was only half scolding. He'd known Ty most of his life, and he'd only been in love one time. Seeing his affection for

Hector should have made Will exultant, except Hector was his little brother, which ripped at his guts even though he'd had months to prepare for this. Was that feeling fear and worry or something else Will was unwilling to decipher?

Hector had the audacity to laugh as Ty said something.

So enmeshed was he in his emotional turmoil, Will lost the train of conversation. It probably didn't matter. Something to do with the best place to hie off for a quick fuck, most likely.

"Hello, gentlemen." Mary swished into the room, all femininity and silk and lightness. She smiled at Ty and Hector scrambling to cover their naked chests. Hector gasped, then moved slower. Ty helped him slip into a shirt.

"My dear Hector," Mary said, "has Wentworth finally remembered the two of you are perfect together?"

Will's mouth dropped open, and he was certain Ty's would have too if not for all his training to be an emotionless aristocrat.

When Hector smiled, Mary said, "It's bloody well about time. I'll lock the door, shall I?"

"Damn good someone has some sense in this family," Will grumbled as he put his armload of seduction items on the floor. "Wentworth, a moment?" He nodded toward the curtained windows and stomped away, Ty following.

Ty clasped Will's shoulder. "Will, I—"

Will spun and stood toe to toe with Ty. "You have been hovering around Hector's coattails for months. Every time you are in port, I find myself tripping over your sorry arse. I want to know right now what your intentions are." He took a deep breath and then lowered his rising voice. "Haven't you done enough damage to my family?"

Ty did not flinch or back down. He looked Will in the eye and said, "I plan to keep him, and I plan to keep him safe. Do not try to stop us."

"Hector can make up his own mind who to be with."

"He has chosen me."

"Then God forbid you hurt him again."

Ty smiled. "Never. Never again, Will." He stuck out his hand.

Will decided to accept the peace offering.

They turned and joined Mary and Hector, who stood only inches apart, sharing a wide-eyed, worried expression.

Finally, Hector broke the silence. "You truly have nothing to say? I mean, you won't attempt to lock me up to keep me away from Wentworth?"

"You've lived up to your name these past few months, little brother, and proved you are grown and brave beyond compare. You can make your own decisions. Just be careful."

Hector smiled like an idiot.

What the hell. Had he never complimented Hector before? Thinking back, perhaps not often. He would remember to do so in the future.

He turned to Ty, still not finished, but that would be a much more private discussion. "I suppose I'd better become used to having you underfoot from now on."

Ty looked at Hector with a lasciviousness that made Will squirm.

"Now get out of my house and take your perverted thoughts somewhere else. I will come by your town house tomorrow to check on my brother's well-being and to give you the rest of my thoughts on the matter. Off you go. I was in the middle of planning my own seduction."

"Will?" Mary said, placing her warm, slender hand on his chest.

God, I love this woman.

Hector and Ty laughed as they finished dressing and escaped the room.

Mary wrapped her arms around him as she watched them depart. "Isn't love a beautiful thing?"

He sighed and shook his head. "If I were convinced it is love."

"It is, my dear. Of that, I am certain." She spun and perused the room.

"Now, what plans did you have for this blanket?"

Chapter Twenty-Six

Hector bounded into the darkened carriage, then sucked in a breath and let it out slowly, waiting for the ripping pain to start. But it did not, and he was damn delighted.

Once inside, he sat in the rear-facing seat.

The coach tilted when Wentworth put his weight on the step, but he didn't enter. For a moment he stood half inside, half outside the vehicle. He stared at Hector and then, his mind apparently made up, he stepped inside and sat beside him.

Hector held his breath and waited for a second, and then Wentworth grasped his hand with a strength that suggested heaven and earth depended on this contact.

"Hector."

"Wentworth." They spoke at the same time.

"Hector, call me Ty."

Hector's shock must have been obvious since he smacked his head against the padded seat back.

Wentworth turned to him, a half smile showing in the dim lamplight.

Shaking his head, Hector recalled the set down given a year prior when Wentworth told him not to call him Ty. Hector said honestly, "I don't think I can."

"It would mean much to me if you could."

This time he shook his head in a visceral response he had no control over. "What I should have said, is I don't want to. I will never call you that." His voice sounded tight and constricted. "That is what Will calls you."

"Yes, but I would like for you to as well."

"I believe, Wentworth, that I would rather eat dirt than call you by the name your first love calls you."

Wentworth's eyes flicked left but came back to focus on Hector. "Maybe in time—"

"When hell runs out of fire." He spewed the words with more heat than intended, then took a deep breath and tried to ease the strain in his shoulders.

Wentworth laughed. "All right, you win. I will not push the issue. Perhaps one day you will see fit to grant me a pet name that will mean even more to both of us."

"I've given you plenty of pet names throughout my adult life, but I'm not certain you would appreciate any of them."

Wentworth gave an aristocratic snort. "I am certain." He drummed his fingers against the side of the carriage. "Given time, I plan to make you forget those ugly memories."

Hector gave his own snort, not quite as aristocratic and with much more sarcasm.

They sat in silence, listening to the carriage creak as it rocked at a slow pace. Hector longed to be out of the city, speeding along country roads, breathing fresh air and the smell of summer crops.

"Hector, I did not bring this up before. Not until you had some distance from the event. Did Will tell you about Jonathan?"

"About him trying to hurt me? Yes."

"Kill you, Hector. He tried to kill you." Wentworth paused as if the memory was too painful.

"I know. Will told me everything."

"Did he tell you how Jonathan died?"

He opened one of the shades and looked out at the lamplit streets. "Someone stabbed him during the commotion."

Wentworth stiffened beside him but said nothing.

"Funny that I'm not surprised. What surprises me is that I was able to be with a man who could kill me without a qualm. That will give me nightmares for years, I'm afraid."

"I am terribly sorry this happened to you, Hector. If I could change the past, I would make this all go away." Reaching over, Wentworth grasped his other hand.

Hector could feel rough skin where countless sailing ropes had burned Wentworth's palms. He turned the hand over and slowly stroked the raised skin. "Seems you are determined to mar your elegance." The shared touch turned to boil the simmer of desire he always felt around this man.

Hector let go of one hand and rubbed Wentworth's thigh, but before desire consumed him, he had to know whether he would get relief or remain frustrated like so many times since his injury. "Are you taking me somewhere to toy with me or to fuck me?"

Wentworth laughed, the sound a warm, sensuous caress. "My dear," he said, reaching across Hector to close the shade and then maneuvering to his knees on the carriage floor. "You are a resilient soul, to be sure, but your injuries were too severe for fornication. You needed time to heal, and it almost proved to be the end of me." Spreading Hector's legs, he fitted himself between them and ran his hands up both thighs, which turned Hector's half-mast erection into full sail.

Damn.

"Now that I know you are healed, I cannot wait long enough to have you at my town house. I have been denied this beautiful body for months. Your lovely prick will be pumping in my mouth before the carriage stops."

The zing of lust and emotion was so fast, so intense, it felt like fear. The hair prickled on his arms and the back of his neck, and Hector could hardly breathe. "God, but I missed you while you were on patrol."

"And I missed you, Hector. Before we arrive, I want to give you this." Wentworth reached into his pocket and pulled out a small sealed note. Very gently, he turned over Hector's hand and placed it on the flat of his palm.

"What the deuce…?"

"I am done letting fear and guilt dictate my actions, Hector. I will work hard for your forgiveness, and I want you in my future. Open it."

He did. The previous surge of fear turned to pure panic. He would not let himself be fooled again. What did the declaration on the paper mean?

Dearest Hector,
 Know that I am truly sorry and plan to spend the
rest of my days making up for being an arse.
 Eternal love,
 Wentworth

He swallowed the burning blockage in his throat. It couldn't possibly mean what he had once hoped for. Couldn't possibly mean a future with Wentworth. Couldn't mean lasting love.

He read the short note, then slapped the paper closed.

"An apology. Oh, jolly good, I'll use this to dry my tears when you tire of me again."

"Let me clarify, since you are resigned to skepticism. I am extraordinarily proud of you, Hector. I do not plan to hide that fact ever again. From myself or from anyone else. Although I might not flaunt my feelings either." His voice barely filled the enclosed space. "The apology is on paper for you to see or to show me whenever I act like a bastard. It is a reminder for me to behave and to remind you that I love you and no one else."

"Lovely speech, but. What. Does. This. Mean?" He waved the paper around, emphasizing each word.

Wentworth sighed. Kneeling like that, sitting back on crossed boots, his low back arched, Wentworth appeared submissive, like an altar boy ready to receive penance. No, not ready for—looking forward to receiving his penance. It was likely the most provocative thing Hector had ever seen.

He was ready to take Wentworth then and there, forcibly if needed. Anything to pump all his frustration and lust out into Wentworth's tight, shivering hole. He wiped sweat off his forehead. God. His balls were blue, and he needed release. Soon.

Slowly Wentworth raised his head. Even in the dim light, Hector could see his intense gaze. "It means as little or as much as you desire."

Hector froze, his erection withering as fear flooded him. *Is this a passing phase for my viscount?* He had to be sure. He could not live through another broken heart. Trembling, he asked the question he was afraid to have answered. "Forever? And when you once again feel guilty over something, or decide it is time to marry and get an heir?"

Wentworth looked down again, slid his hands slowly up until his thumbs pressed the cloth at Hector's groin where leg met torso. He moved his thumbs back and forth.

Gooseflesh started on Hector's skin at the intimate touch, and his flagging erection regained strength.

Staring directly into Hector's eyes, Wentworth hissed, frustrated, as if the words had boiled up into steam inside him for years. "I have a few things I still need to work out in my thinking. I want you to help me work through them."

"I believe your problems may be beyond help," Hector said.

"Pay attention if you will, rambunctious one. I have more to tell you."

"Yes, your lordship."

Wentworth laughed, even though moments ago their discussion had been painfully serious. "Peter's eldest son will inherit. I just left my solicitor's office. I asked him to draw up the paperwork to make it formal." He cleared his throat. "Tomorrow before we leave for Kent, I will sign it, along with the paperwork giving you five hundred a year when I die."

"What the devil—"

He held up a hand. "Let me finish, Hector. Then you can berate me all you want." Before continuing, he took a long breath and rotated his shoulders.

"I wish I were a good man. I am not, but I hope you can accept me and the half good that lies beneath my rib cage, as I have no intention of ever marrying a woman, and, yes, I will touch you and only you. Until I take my last breath. I was wrong before, and I want to make this very clear now. You are the single most important thing in my life. Past, present, and future."

Hector blinked fast to keep the damn tears from falling. Leaning over, he touched his lips to Wentworth's and found his kiss pliant and tender. No longer the aloof aristocrat avoiding Hector's kiss, this time Wentworth's breath caught and his frame shivered.

Hector quite liked the change.

Wentworth pulled away, stared at Hector's lips, then moved in again, deepening the kiss, delving in with lust, tongue, and spirit. When he drew away, taking with him half the carriage's warmth, he whispered in a Sunday morning voice, "You taste like spring. Similar, but different. Why did I not notice before?" Then he reached for another, gentler kiss. "I love you, Hector."

The temperature in the carriage shot to Saharan proportions.

He really loves me. Oh yes, Hector definitely liked the new Wentworth. No, actually, a better term would be *loved.*

❖

Wentworth was mortified. He'd just declared his intentions for Hector, and the blasted man sat there saying nothing, one lovely, infernal eyebrow cocked.

He acted fast to take the focus off his embarrassment. "Hector, open your falls. I told you I would suck you before we left the coach, and the ride is nearly over, so do hurry."

He undid his falls in record time but sported an insolent, crooked smile.

Wentworth was about to kiss the insolence out of that smile when he saw the long prick inches from his face. Forgetting about embarrassment, forgetting about mortification, he buried his face in Hector's pubic hair and took a long, full breath of the humid, musky smell of sunshine, earth, and male that was all Hector's.

Why had he not noticed the much richer fragrance than Will's sun, salt, and man? Hector tasted like sun-warmed spring earth, while Will tasted like a lonely, barren beach.

"Damn, Wentworth. Damn." Hector surged up, his cock rubbing Wentworth's cheek. "I love you."

Wentworth drove his nose even deeper and captured the smell of heaven...no, not heaven...*home*. The smell of home.

At last. He was home.

❖

Hector pulled Wentworth's hair to get his attention. "Suck me, my love."

Wentworth stared into his eyes as he sank his perfect mouth on Hector's straining cock.

"Oh God, that feels…" Hector clenched his fist in Wentworth's ebony hair and rocked up into the sublime warmth. He'd been so close to coming for the past half hour, this amazing encounter would not last long. He pumped his hips and whispered, "Touch yourself. I want to see you come."

Cloth rustled, and then came the sound of flesh against flesh. The scent of the translucent liquid pearl at the tip of Hector's cock, coupled with the moist slide of tongue on his shaft, sent him into ecstasy. He moaned and closed his eyes, fully experiencing the shattering feel of his body pumping seed into Wentworth's mouth.

When Hector was able to open his eyes again, it was too late to watch Wentworth spend. Wentworth breathed hard around the softening cock in his mouth, hands still, stiffened shoulders now loosened. How could anyone look exquisite no matter what they did?

Reaching down to pull Wentworth back onto the seat, Hector said, "Tonight I plan to take your arse."

Wentworth's eyes went wide. He straightened his clothing, opened one shutter, and picked up the note. "If you keep this and put it someplace safe, I will do anything you ask of me tonight."

"Anything?"

"Yes." He handed the letter back to Hector, who held the sheet up to the light, turning it for better illumination. He squinted in the waning light, reading the words again.

He swallowed the constriction seizing up his throat as he folded and placed the paper in his coat pocket, close to his heart. It felt right there, somehow warming him from the inside out. In fact, everything felt perfect.

"Close the shutter, love. I want to show you that I accept your apology."

CHAPTER TWENTY-SEVEN

Five days later

"I am very glad we stayed in London," Hector said as he stretched in a pool of morning sunlight that reached the rumpled bed. The sheet fell from his chest, exposing a faint scar that stretched across his ribs below one nipple, marring the pristine skin.

Wentworth flinched, remembering nearly losing Hector. "How are you this morning, and why are you glad we stayed in London?"

Hector rolled toward him and smiled. "Because I did not realize how comfortable a bed can be." He sighed dramatically. "It would be much better, however, if I hadn't awakened alone."

"You were not alone. I am right over here, catching up on correspondence."

Looking at the desk across the room where Wentworth and a tea tray waited for him, Hector said, "That is a full fifteen feet too far away."

Laughing, Wentworth went to the bed, toed off his shoes, and slipped under the fine green quilt to hold Hector close. "There is a breakfast tray. Would you like anything to break your fast?"

"Hmm, not yet. I'm just barely awake."

"You had bad dreams last night."

"Not as bad as the night before." He shrugged and nestled his head on Wentworth's chest.

The fine linen lawn shirt Wentworth wore was so thin, Hector's morning stubble poked through and tickled. Wentworth rubbed one strong, bare shoulder, trying not to get aroused. They made love many different ways and quite frequently this week, but he still had to fight his growing desire. Hector could get his rod hard just by looking at him a certain way.

God, what had he done to deserve such happiness? Perhaps he had done nothing and luck had simply landed in his bed. Wentworth kissed the top of that curly, dark head.

"It helps knowing you are next to me," Hector said. "When I wake from one of those dreams, I feel your arms around me, and I can relax back into slumber." He twirled one finger across Wentworth's belly.

Blood rushed straight to his cock, so he stilled Hector's hand with his own.

"Thank you for letting me stay here," Hector said. "I'm certain they will go away with time, especially now the pain in my chest is gone. I should stay at my own rooms, though. For appearances, if nothing more." He pointed at the closed door for emphasis. "I shall go back to my rooms, let you get on with your business. I…I hope to see you often, however, if you are—"

"Oh, do stop that, Hector. I do not want you to leave. I hope you will stay in my bed every day when I'm not at sea. In fact, under the guise of economy, I think you should give up your rooms and move in with me. We are lifelong friends. No one will think anything is out of the ordinary. Friends do that sort of thing."

"The servants will start spreading gossip since you lock the door to your sitting room as well as your bedchamber."

"Yes, that situation is a bit more delicate, so I put some thought into our problem. We shall ensconce you in the room down the hall, and tell the servants that since you suffer from nightmares, everyone but you and I must avoid this wing at all times unless called. I hope you do not mind being the scapegoat, but if I suddenly claim to start having bad dreams, I am afraid the doctor will be summoned."

Hector rubbed his face against Wentworth's chest like a puppy in sun-warmed grass. "If it keeps me close to you, then I have no complaints."

"Good. We can work out all the details later. Right now, I think you should eat something."

"No, I'd rather make good use of this bed while I have you in it." Hector started unbuttoning Wentworth's shirt with deft fingers.

That simple act, the light brush against his chest, had Wentworth's rod at full sail. He lifted Hector's chin with one finger and kissed him deeply and thoroughly, enjoying what he'd stupidly refused before. He would never again pass on the opportunity to taste his lips.

They worked together to strip Wentworth of his clothes, never completely breaking contact with each other. The position was awkward, making a simple task take three times longer than necessary, but they both needed the closeness. Wentworth at least knew he needed the intimacy.

At last he was as naked as his lover. Hector's bed-warm skin was smooth, his cock hard, bumping and rubbing against Wentworth's thigh as talented fingers teased one nipple.

"My ribs are fully healed. I think it will be fine if you fuck me," Hector said.

Wentworth's body surged with arousal at the words, but

as enticing as that idea was, he needed something else. Every day he remembered how wonderful the experience had been when Hector fucked him, and he greatly desired to repeat the event.

"Actually, I rather think I would prefer for you to make love to me. Seems I like it more than I ever imagined."

Hector sucked in a deep breath and trembled. "With pleasure." He kissed the tip of Wentworth's rod. "Turn over, then."

"No. No, I want to see you, kiss you when you take me." He laughed softly. What a sentimental fool he'd turned into.

"Oh yes," Hector whispered as he reached for the bedside table and retrieved the oil.

Several moments and only a few mishaps later—one elbow to the chin and a knee to the belly—they were situated with Hector lying on his back and Wentworth straddling him.

Rising on one foot and one knee to allow Hector easy access to his arse, Wentworth prepared for the initial pain as Hector slipped one, then two, then three fingers inside. The preparation was necessary, but not his favorite part.

When his body relaxed and the fingers slid smoothly, Wentworth began to enjoy the stretching sensation and the bump against that sensitive spot as he panted. "I am amply prepared. Get on with it," he snapped. He was more than ready, and at that moment he would shatter into a thousand pieces if Hector did not enter him soon.

Hector withdrew and steadied his rod while Wentworth positioned himself over his beautiful, flushed cock. His opening clenched once again as he lowered himself down on it, so he took a deep breath and let it out. His anus relaxed, and slowly, deliberately, opened for the penetration on that wonderful iron and satin prick.

"God, that…" He swallowed the rest of the words on a gasp. The sensation of being filled, the look of pure lust on Hector's handsome face, the weeks of waiting…it all became too much. He sat quickly all the way until fully seated.

His arse trembled. Each grasp and release reverberated through his body and was almost enough to make him spend. Gritting his teeth, he got himself under control.

"Do something, Wentworth, before I die of frustration." Hector rocked up, sending a sensation like an electric shock through his body, and Wentworth could not keep still if his life depended on it. He lifted and slammed down, over and over.

There was no finesse, no trying to angle himself so that hard cock of Hector's hit his sensitive spot. There was only lust, love, and a bone-deep pleasure that sent him to his climax long before he wanted. He closed his eyes and yelled his completion.

Bliss ebbed and flowed through Wentworth like a full-moon tide. Slowly, he fell against Hector, both of them still breathless. He was embarrassed to realize two things. One, he came without stimulus to his cock because he'd pounded poor Hector so hard and fast, he'd never let go of the bedcovers. Two, he's been so caught up in his own pleasure, he did not even know if Hector found his release.

What a selfish oaf he was. He lifted off Hector and winced when the softening cock slipped out from his arse. Well, that answered his question.

Hector lay very still, eyes closed.

"I hurt you. I am such a—"

"No." Hector opened those big, beautiful dark eyes. "You did not hurt me. What you did was send me around the world and back. God, I have not felt that wonderful in…Well, maybe

I've never felt that good." He chuckled and closed his eyes again.

Looking at Hector beside him in his bed, he knew he was the luckiest man in London. Hell, probably in all of England. He pulled Hector into an embrace and leaned in to plunder his warm lips.

"I believe I will stow away on your *Dragon* when you must go back, so I can use your body for my pleasure every morning and evening."

"It is ill advised to let this incident go to your head, Sprout."

"Don't—"

He laughed. "A deal, then. I will not call you Sprout if you remember not to get above yourself." With that, he smacked Hector on the thigh and left the bed.

"Where are you off to?"

"To get you something to eat. You have about half a stone to put back on your frame." Wentworth dressed quickly and then went to see if the tea was still warm.

Hector's stomach growled in agreement. "You know, I've been thinking."

"Terrible habit to get into."

Hector lobbed a pillow at him. It missed.

"What I was about to say is, I would like to spend a few days sailing with you. Learn about seafaring so I can better understand what you do. So I can talk about maritime things with you." He slipped out of bed and found an elegant sapphire-blue dressing gown that made his rumpled hair seem that much more disreputable. "Would you let me do that? Sail with you on a short trip?"

"For you, dear, anything. And I would enjoy learning about your porcelain business. I am impressed with your unique endeavor and the fact that you increased profit by fifty percent in the past year. How did you manage that?"

"Questions later, love. Let us never again waste time. And right now, I need you."

He never got around to checking if the tea was still warm, but it did not really matter since the bed was.

EPILOGUE

Summer 1810, a few miles east of London

"What a perfect day," Hector said for the third time that afternoon. The weather was sunny and warm, the Somerville estate was green and festive for the occasion, and the company was sublime."

Wentworth had no complaints. He lounged on a blanket, watching Hector tickle Pug. "Best be careful. If you get her too stirred up, she will revisit the cake she ate not fifteen minutes ago."

Hector laughed. "Tickling won't make anyone up their accounts." He gave his niece an additional round of torment, then lay on the blanket. Pug gasped for breath next to her baby brother, whom Hector had given the awful but appropriate nickname Boulder. The baby was large and round and slept all the time, rarely moving. He was a startling contrast to his sister, who was in constant motion, just like her uncle.

Mary and Will were somewhere near the front of the house, bidding farewell to the rest of the guests while he and Hector enjoyed some time alone with the children.

Hector, arms behind his head, looked at the sky, while Pug prodded her brother with one pink shoe. "It was a nice party, but I must say I'm glad everyone is gone. I've been meaning to ask you something."

That was a surprise. Normally Hector blurted out what was on his mind. If he had to wait for the appropriate moment, this was serious. Wentworth sat up and moved Pug's foot away from Horatio Forsythe Hector Somerville's face. God, but he needed to have a word with Will about his choice of names. He had happily agreed to be Boulder's godfather, but that was before he realized what the child would be christened.

Boulder snuffled in his sleep, and Pug leaned over to stare at him, just two inches from his face. It gave Wentworth a headache just thinking about focusing on an object that close. "Children are rather interesting to watch—have you noticed that?"

"Indeed, and that brings me to my idea."

"Oh no. I will not like this, will I?"

"Let's just say you might have to think about it before commenting."

Wentworth slipped closer to Hector so he could touch his arm. He was, however, careful to keep the children between them for appearances. "Tell me, dear."

Hector shivered. "God, I adore it when you call me dear."

"You are. Always."

Hector rolled onto his side. "I love you too, Wentworth."

"Perhaps you will call me Tyler, then."

"What? But you hate that name."

"Yes, well. Wentworth just doesn't roll off the tongue when in the same sentence as *love*. Perhaps if you use Tyler enough, I will learn to appreciate my given name."

Dark eyes shining, Hector gave him a quivering smile.

Wentworth asked, "When can we pass these tiny humans off to their parents and sneak up to our rooms?"

"Not for a while, I believe. So, let me get back to what I have been trying to say."

"Yes, please do, dear. I cannot wait to hear what mischief you have swimming around in your beautiful head."

Hector smiled and gently snagged Pug before she could escape the blanket, then plopped her back in the middle. He shook his finger at her. "Behave and stay on the blanket, or I will tickle you again."

"No," she screamed, but then ruined her protest by giggling, which of course spurred a new attack of tickles. Five minutes later, Hector was cleaning regurgitated cake off Pug's pretty pink dress and soothing her tears with funny stories.

"Next time Will and Mary have a christening, I believe we should be on the *Dragon*, bound for a mundane battle somewhere in the Mediterranean. What do you say?"

Laughing, Hector wiped sweat from his brow. "I think that is a wonderful idea."

"I have thought about it, you know."

"Thought about…?"

"Fostering. Having children underfoot. They do add excitement in one's life, do they not?"

Hector beamed at him. "They do. They do indeed."

"My first thought is that it is right for us. Not now, not while I am away so much and there is trouble brewing. I do not see you enough as it is. You tell me often enough how selfish I am. I want all your time for myself."

"Damn, when will my blasted brother finish with his guests? I want you, in bed, clothes off, skin on display for my pleasure." Hector looked at that moment as if he were about to climb over the children and ravish him.

"Unkl. Don feel goud." Pug looked about to cry.

Hector whisked her up. "Don't worry, my little pup. I'll

take you to your mother." He mumbled, "Stay right there. I will be back soon," and he was off.

Wentworth and Boulder lazed in the weak sunlight. He occasionally shook the boy to make certain he was still alive. Each time, he snorted and went right back to sleep.

When footsteps sounded on the fresh grass, Wentworth said, "I told you not to tickle her that much."

Instead of a crisp tenor, a rough voice answered, "I'm certain Margaret will be fine. Mary and Hector are cooing over her as if they know what they are about."

He sat bolt upright. "Will?"

"I came to take Horatio up for his nap."

Wentworth laughed. "Nap? He has slept all day."

"Yes, but it was a fitful sleep with all the noise and interruptions."

"Heaven forbid someone interrupt his afternoon nap. It might interfere with his late-afternoon nap."

Will smiled at Boulder. "Thank you," he said to Wentworth.

The hair on the back of his neck rose. "For what?"

Will looked at him. Those knowing black eyes drilled into his deepest secrets. "For making Hector happy, for watching the children today, for once again being a dear friend. I missed you, Ty."

Wentworth looked at the clouds building in the sky. It would be a cool evening, and they might even have rain. "I believe I should be the one thanking you—for giving me back an extended family, for trusting I will not turn into an abomination, for trusting me with your children, for forgiving me, and for blessing my relationship with Hector." His voice grew thick, so he stopped blabbering.

Will squeezed his knee—the warmth seeping through Wentworth's trousers did not stir his cock like it would have years before—and then stooped to pick up his boy.

"Oof, you are a big boy, aren't you, my good-natured baby? I think he is saving all his energy for growing. But don't let his gentle nature fool you. He will be a man to reckon with when he grows into all this heft."

"I am certain of that. With a father and mother like his, there cannot possibly be any other outcome."

"When do you sail again?"

"Too soon. Much too soon. I have been assured that we will be assigned to channel patrol. If that holds true, I plan to ask Hector if he will stay in Portsmouth so I can see him every week or two. I'm not certain he will leave his business, though. He gets so much enjoyment running the whole ugly… ugly…"

"Monstrosity?"

"Quite."

"You know, I've not once regretted my choice to become a landlubber. You might think about it. There's no disgrace in turning in your commission. You have an exemplary record. Maybe it's time to let someone else rule the seas."

Wentworth smiled to himself and wondered what he would do if he never again had a ship under his feet to command. "An excellent notion, Will. I shall think on it. Seems I have quite a lot to think on just now. Ah, there is Hector."

"It is getting late. I'll have tea sent to your rooms. No hurry if you don't mind cold tea."

"Will, I…" He tugged at his shirtsleeve. "I should not ask, but for some reason I feel I have a right to know. The offer, the one you made during the fortnight… Well, what was on the table?"

Will looked away sharply. "I don't really know, to be honest. It was just that you had always been there, always my best friend, often more than that. I suppose there were several reasons why I did not want you and Hector together." He laughed without mirth, bouncing Boulder gently. "Seems I'm not such an upstanding gentleman as I thought if I let jealousy control me."

"Ah. Just a man after all." He smiled at Will, who smiled back.

Will left, and halfway to the manor exchanged a few words with Hector. It was not long before Hector sat next to Wentworth, bumping his shoulder. "Is all well?" Hector asked.

"Yes, just contemplating the future."

"And does the future look good for us?"

He took Hector's hand and stared into his tea-colored eyes. "My love, my spring, the future looks bright indeed. Let's go upstairs for tea, and I will show you how I envision it."

"You know, I purchased some violet silk curtain ties at the market last week. Brought them along, thinking how decadent you would look trussed up to my brother's guest bed. You were so wanton the last time I strapped you down. Thought we'd try it again."

The surge of desire at the thought of being rendered totally helpless for Hector's pleasure surprised him once again. And he was behind the idea fully, totally, and erectly.

He was halfway to his feet when Hector smiled and said, "Bet I can make it to the guest chamber before you." Then the imp was off and away before Wentworth even realized a race was under way. He bellowed, "You cheated, brat!" As he ran down the hill to the manor house, his mind summoned up all the delicious ways he would make Hector pay for rushing the gun...just as soon as Hector released him from the new silk bindings.

AUTHOR'S NOTE

There are a few historical figures in this novel, but most of the characters are completely our creation. Please forgive small rearrangements of some historical facts in order to give the characters a story they could be proud of participating in.

And, yes, I did purposefully have Wentworth misrepresent what his given name means. It seemed more fun that way.

I became interested in traumatic memory suppression when I realized that years after a distressing event, Lake would mention something about that time frame, and I'd say, "Damn, I forgot all about that." Wondering why I would forget something that memorable gave me the idea for Wentworth. However, I only forgot one event; Wentworth suffered three highly traumatic events, causing him quite a few holes in his personal timeline.

I hope you love Wentworth's story, and if you're interested in traumatic memory suppression, there is plenty of reading on the Internet.

Enjoy!

About the Author

Stephanie Lake is the pen name for a husband/wife team who enjoy writing happy endings and steamy middles. We write historical and contemporary LGBTQ and mainstream romance. Inspiration for our stories comes from living in seven different countries and traveling around the world. Wherever we wander, our beloved four-legged family member is not far away. We'd love to hear from you, so drop us a line at SLake255@gmail.com, or visit our Facebook page at https://www.facebook.com/StephanieLakeRomance.

Books Available From Bold Strokes Books

His Brother's Viscount by Stephanie Lake. Hector Somerville wants to rekindle his illicit love affair with Viscount Wentworth, but he must overcome one problem: Wentworth still loves Hector's brother. (978-1-63555-805-0)

The Dubious Gift of Dragon Blood by J. Marshall Freeman. One day Crispin is a lonely high school student—the next he is fighting a war in a land ruled by dragons, his otherworldly boyfriend at his side. (978-1-63555-725-1)

Quake City by St John Karp. Can Andre find his best friend Amy before the night devolves into a nightmare of broken hearts, malevolent drag queens, and spontaneous human combustion? Or has it always happened this way, every night, at Aunty Bob's Quake City Club? (978-1-63555-723-7)

Death Overdue by David S. Pederson. Did Heath turn to murder in an alcohol-induced haze to solve the problem of his blackmailer, or was it someone else who brought about a death overdue? (978-1-63555-711-4)

Every Summer Day by Lee Patton. Meant to celebrate every summer day, Luke's journal instead chronicles a love affair as fast-moving and possibly as fatal as his brother's brain tumor. (978-1-63555-706-0)

Everyday People by Louis Barr. When film star Diana Danning hires private eye Clint Steele to find her son, Clint turns to his former West Point barracks mate, and ex-buddy with benefits, Mars Hauser to lend his cyber espionage and digital black ops skills to the case.(978-1-63555-698-8)

Cirque des Freaks and Other Tales of Horror by Julian Lopez. Explore the pleasure of horror in this compilation that delivers like the horror classics...good ole tales of terror. (978-1-63555-689-6)

Royal Street Reveillon by Greg Herren. In this Scotty Bradley mystery, someone is killing the stars of a reality show, and it's up to Scotty Bradley and the boys to find out who. (978-1-63555-545-5)

Death Takes a Bow by David S. Pederson. Alan Keys takes part in a local stage production, but when the leading man is murdered, his partner Detective Heath Barrington is thrust into the limelight to find the killer. (978-1-63555-472-4)

Accidental Prophet by Bud Gundy. Days after his grandmother dies, Drew Morten learns his true identity and finds himself racing against time to save civilization from the apocalypse. (978-1-63555-452-6)

In Case You Forgot by Fredrick Smith and Chaz Lamar. Zaire and Kenny, two newly single, Black, queer, and socially aware men, start again—in love, career, and life—in the West Hollywood neighborhood of LA. (978-1-63555-493-9)

Counting for Thunder by Phillip Irwin Cooper. A struggling actor returns to the Deep South to manage a family crisis but finds love and ultimately his own voice as his mother is regaining hers for possibly the last time. (978-1-63555-450-2)

Survivor's Guilt and Other Stories by Greg Herren. Award-winning author Greg Herren's short stories are finally pulled together into a single collection, including the Macavity Award–nominated title story and the first-ever Chanse MacLeod short story. (978-1-63555-413-7)

Exit Plans for Teenage Freaks by 'Nathan Burgoine. Cole always has a plan—especially for escaping his small-town reputation as "that kid who was kidnapped when he was four"—but when he teleports to a museum, it's time to face facts: it's possible he's a total freak after all. (978-1-163555-098-6)

Death Checks In by David S. Pederson. Despite Heath's promises to Alan to not get involved, Heath can't resist investigating a shopkeeper's murder in Chicago, which dashes their plans for a romantic weekend getaway. (978-1-163555-329-1)

Of Echoes Born by 'Nathan Burgoine. A collection of queer fantasy short stories set in Canada from Lambda Literary Award finalist 'Nathan Burgoine. (978-1-63555-096-2)

The Lurid Sea by Tom Cardamone. Cursed to spend eternity on his knees, Nerites is having the time of his life. (978-1-62639-911-2)

www.ingramcontent.com/pod-product-compliance
Lightning Source LLC
Chambersburg PA
CBHW030513020726
47494CB00004B/1078